A Freedom Such as Heaven Intended

Heaven Intended (#4)

A Novel

By Amanda Lauer

Full Quiver Publishing
Pakenham ON

This book is a work of fiction. Although the setting for this novel takes place in the 19th century, some of the names, characters and incidents are products of the author's imagination. Real events and characters are used fictitiously.

A Freedom Such as Heaven Intended
copyright 2021
by Amanda Lauer

Published by Full Quiver Publishing
PO Box 244
Pakenham, Ontario K0A 2X0

ISBN Number: 978-1-987970-31-9

Printed and bound in the USA

Background, cover model and back cover
All courtesy of Brad Birkholz
Cover design: James Hrkach, Amanda Lauer

NATIONAL LIBRARY OF CANADA
CATALOGUING IN PUBLICATION

Published by FQ Publishing
A Division of Innate Productions

Endorsements

Amanda Lauer's latest 'Heaven Intended' book follows a group of runaway slaves as they begin a perilous and uncertain journey to freedom. Plenty of historical detail leaves the reader immersed in the world of Civil War-era Georgia, as characters struggle to discern whether to risk their lives in the service of others. Faith plays a role, in often surprising ways, in the twists and turns of the plot of this compelling novel.
Barb Szyszkiewicz, author of *The Handy Little Guide to Prayer*

My favorite of the series. 'A Freedom Such as Heaven Intended' is the first of Lauer's acclaimed Civil War YA novels to feature an African American: Alice, the mysterious fugitive discovered by Brigid in 'A Life Such as Heaven Intended,' tells the story of her own enslavement, a tragic-but-royal past, and the tiny infant she must care for as she attempts the heroic journey to freedom. Catholic, law-abiding First Lieutenant Marshall Kent must choose between his religious beliefs and his sworn duty to defend the Constitution of the Confederate States."
Jeanie Egolf, author, publisher

The Heaven Intended series continues with this fourth tale of intrigue, deception, compassion and love. I have been a huge fan of this series, so I anxiously awaited the newest book. It was worth the wait. Lauer seamlessly intertwines fascinating bits of history into her compelling story. A Freedom Such as Heaven Intended adds a captivating new dimension to this hard-to-put-down novel.
Leslea Wahl, author

Once again, a great Civil War novel: lively and lovable characters, an engaging plot and just the right amount of history and romance. The honest and true Catholic faith of Alice and Marshall makes their storylines interesting and enjoyable. An amazing read!
Sophie Habsburg-Lothringen

To Margaret Nicole, whose birth earned me the honorary title Dr. Grandma Baby Catcher

Chapter I
Wednesday, May 25, 1864
Dallas, Georgia

She kept a steady hand on the reins as she made her way through the streets of Dallas, the gig pulled by a single horse. Doing her best to keep a casual demeanor, Alice's eyes swept from one side of the residential neighborhood street to the other, searching for her mark.

After a wet spring, the lawns in front of the stately homes were lush and green, making it even more difficult to find the unique sage-colored plant. While the vegetation she sought was called a green rose, in actuality, it was a mutated rose with sepals instead of petals, so it didn't have the appearance of the typical flower of that genus.

Green roses were said to signify rejuvenation of spirit and fertility. *Rejuvenation I can take; fertility, no thank you.* Alice rolled her eyes. *That's the last thing that I need to enhance in my life.*

She resumed her search. Turning the corner onto another quiet street, Alice perused the front yards of the houses. Still nothing. The sound of an approaching horse caused her to snap her head back to see who was coming her way.

Sitting ramrod straight on the seat of the conveyance, she self-consciously tugged her crocheted gloves up to the bottom of the sleeves of her day dress, leaving as little skin visible as possible.

As the horse and rider neared, Alice saw a young

man, perhaps a few years her senior, bedecked in the uniform of a Confederate soldier. No stars on his collar, so he wasn't high brass. The bars sewn on his epaulets indicated that he was an officer, though. Having had scant interaction with military personnel, Alice wasn't sure what rank three bars signified.

When the horse and rider came close, Alice politely nodded her head toward the man in greeting and proceeded forward, hoping that he'd continue on his way as well. After driving several more yards, she assumed that she was in the clear.

A moment later, she heard a strong male voice behind her. "Haw," the man said firmly.

Alice's heart sank to her stomach. He'd commanded the animal to turn left, no doubt to follow after her gig. Haughtily, she tilted her head up and willed an unperturbed expression to settle on her face. A few seconds later, the soldier pulled up next to her.

"Miss, would you be kind enough to stop your vehicle?"

The baritone voice was southern, no doubt about it. But it differed from the accent she was accustomed to hearing in their area.

After a quick sideways glance, which gave her enough chance to see the man's profile, Alice replied. "Of course."

He was quite striking. Rather than putting her at ease, though, his good looks caused her tension to heighten. Over the course of her seventeen years, she'd come to find that a handsome, manly visage most often hid a troublesome core.

"May I help you, sir?" she inquired in the most refined voice that she could muster.

"Pardon me, miss. I've been assigned to patrol these streets. Doing what we can to keep the fine citizens of Dallas safe."

With him staring directly at her, Alice couldn't help but notice his hazel eyes. The color was hauntingly familiar. They were just a shade lighter than Josiah's. The man's neatly trimmed chestnut-colored hair and his long black eyelashes drew her attention as well. If she hadn't known better, she'd have sworn that he was related to the boy. It took considerable willpower to tear her gaze away from him.

"It's a bit concerning that you're out on these streets unescorted, young lady."

His pronouncement nearly brought an eye roll from Alice. *Young lady?* Coming from a man who was — at most — five years older than her, that was rather comical. And his concern about her welfare driving through a sleepy neighborhood seemed a bit contrived.

If the soldier actually had known anything about her, he'd be more anxious for any person seeking to cause her trouble than the other way around. She knew how to defend herself. Thanks to her brother, she also knew how to take a man down with one well-placed kick or a hand chop to the throat.

"Thank you for looking out after my welfare, sir...."

"First Lieutenant Kent. Marshall Kent."

He gave her a smile. There appeared to be no malice brewing below the surface. Regardless, she had just cause to be suspicious.

"Thank you, First Lieutenant *Marshall* Kent," she enunciated. "But I'm just fine. I know my way around this city."

"More than I do, I'd wager, miss..."

His voice trailed off. She should have been prepared for the inquiry but was caught off guard. Alice had been preoccupied staring into his eyes, which exuded nothing but friendliness and sincerity. Something she'd seldom found in men like him.

"...Rose." Considering her mission, it was the first word that came to mind. "Miss Rose," she noted with more assurance.

"Well, Miss *Rose*, you may know this city, but I must warn you that a skirmish is being waged not far from here at New Hope Church. As has been known to happen under such circumstances, riffraff could be scuttling out of the line of fire and heading this way as we speak."

Was this true? Try as Alice did to keep abreast of war news, the only tidbits that she'd been privy to were the whispers amongst the residents of Pecan Hall. The Williams family had been somewhat reticent lately when speaking of the hostilities. *Could this mean that the momentum of the war is turning in a positive direction?*

As much as she'd like to grill the first lieutenant on the topic, she needed to disengage from the conversation — and him — as quickly as she could.

"A battle, so close to Dallas? Oh my," she exclaimed with a hint of feigned distress in her voice. "I had no idea. Of course, I leave politics and war up to the menfolk." She batted her lashes — shaded as they were under the rim of her bonnet — at the first lieutenant. It was a ploy that she'd learned from her half-sister.

He looked at her reassuringly. "Don't you worry your pretty little self, none, Miss Rose. The Confederate Army of Tennessee — under the command of General

Joseph Johnston — stopped Major General William Sherman and General Joseph Hooker's XX Corps dead in their tracks."

The color drained from Alice's face.

Continuing his narrative, First Lieutenant Kent added, "Pardon my French, but the Union Army is said to have called the place a Hell Hole when all was said and done."

French? Alice had to refrain from scoffing. *This man probably wouldn't know French if it bit him in the derriere.*

"This could be just what we need to turn the tide of this war and send the Union Army packing. They can tuck their tails between their legs and skedaddle back to where they came from. Then us Southern states can govern ourselves as we see fit."

This tête-à-tête was nothing short of disheartening. Hoping to wrap things up, Alice addressed the soldier. "I really must be on my way. I would imagine you have more pressing matters to attend to as well...."

"Watching out for the welfare of folks in this district is my primary concern," he replied with a jaunty grin. "May I accompany you to your destination?"

As much as she wanted to continue searching for that elusive green rose, she had to do something to set this obstinate man on another path.

"Actually, now that I've gotten some fresh air, I'm heading over to the dry goods shop. I'll be on my way."

She picked up the reins and slapped the rump of the horse.

"I'm just headed that way myself," said the first lieutenant.

Can't this man take a hint? Alice wondered, gritting

her teeth in frustration.

"Aren't you just the kind one," she replied, pasting a smile on her face.

"Just trying to be the gentleman my mama taught me to be," he retorted, a twinkle in his eye.

They rode a block in silence before the man piped up again. "Here's a shortcut. Let's cut through this alley." He dipped his head to the left.

Alice pulled on one rein to get her horse to follow his. As they trotted along the dirt path, something caught her eye.

The rose! She clapped her hand over her mouth before the word "hallelujah" could tumble out. *Maybe this man isn't so insufferable after all.*

Chapter II

Marshall flung himself off Maximus' back and hurried over to tie Miss Rose's horse to the post in front of the dry goods shop. He then scooted to the side of the vehicle to offer her his hand to help her step down onto the wooden sidewalk.

Such a warm day to be wearing gloves. Obviously, she's a well-bred young lady. Encasing her left hand in his right hand, he surreptitiously ran his thumb over her ring finger, checking to see if it was encircled with a band. Feeling nothing, a smile came to his lips.

He was tempted to show off his chivalrous side and kiss the top of her hand after she disembarked. The young lady had such a regal posture, he felt compelled to present himself as her knight in shining armor.

Not wanting to come off as overdramatic, he refrained, gave her a wink and said instead, "It was a pleasure to meet you, princess."

Miss Rose pulled back as if his sentiment startled her. Then, regaining her composure, she looked directly into his eyes as though she were assessing his character. Thankfully he'd been to Confession this week, or he'd have been squirming under her inspection.

"*Enchantée de faire votre connaissance,*" she replied smoothly.

Willing his jaw to stay shut, Marshall smiled broadly, put his hand on her elbow and escorted her through the door of the business.

Enchantée sounded similar to *enchanted.* Perhaps

he'd piqued her interest as she had his?

Brains and beauty? What man wouldn't be intrigued by that?

Once Miss Rose was securely inside the building, Marshall hopped down from the raised sidewalk and pulled himself up on his mount. He was tempted to bide his time outside the establishment so that he could escort the young lady back to her house. It would be interesting to learn more about her. However, that may appear too forward. A woman of her status needed to be treated just so.

Besides that, a creature that lovely probably fought off suitors every day. Or, at least, every day up until all the men marched off to war. But, even with pickings as slim as they were now, he didn't want to appear to be just another young buck vying for her attention.

Giving a sigh, he made a clicking sound to set the gelding into motion to continue his rounds. As he made his way up and down the streets of the small town, his thoughts wandered back to the captivating Miss Rose.

She seemed a bit aloof, which wasn't the reception that he was used to receiving from the fairer sex. With his sense of humor, he'd always been able to charm the girls in school. Primary school, that was. Once he'd been accepted into The Citadel Military Academy, the only females that he encountered were cooks and the wash women. None of the young men had a desire to woo those spinsters whose job descriptions allegedly included curtailing the cadets' merriment.

He'd had a field day when he was home on school breaks, though. Young ladies couldn't resist a man in uniform. Back in the day, he'd had his pick of pretty girls to court. Some of them hinted that they wanted to get to know him a bit more intimately, but he'd held back. Maybe it was his traditional Catholic upbringing — the angel on his right shoulder duking it out with the devil on his left shoulder — but he hadn't succumbed to any of their womanly charms, despite their surprisingly conniving ways.

He did have aspirations of finding a wife and starting a family someday, but, at twenty years old, there was still a lot of adventuring that he wanted to do before he settled down.

The outbreak of the Civil War had given him just that opportunity.

By chance, Marshall was an eye witness to the events that set off the whole powder keg. As The Citadel was located in Charleston, officers from the school had spent considerable time in the spring of 1861 assisting with the setup of artillery positions in Charleston's harbor, where Fort Sumter was located.

The fourth-year cadets graduated on April 9, 1861, but many underclassmen were scheduled to stay at the academy the rest of that week to complete their exams before going back to their hometowns for summer break.

The Citadel, like the Arsenal Academy in Columbia, was built in the 1820s as a state arsenal, expressly to ensure that South Carolina was prepared in the event of a slave revolt like the one supposedly planned by Charlestonian Denmark Vesey in 1822.

Vesey, a carpenter and one of the founders of the African Methodist Episcopal Church — the first independent Negro denomination in the United States — had won a lottery and purchased his freedom when he was in his thirties. Even though he was a successful businessman, he had been unable to buy his wife and children out of slavery. People speculated that his disappointment might have led him to become the leader of a revolt against the local slaveholders. The plan was unearthed, and he was executed before the insurrection came to fruition.

In 1842 arsenals throughout the state were consolidated to two institutions, Arsenal Military Academy and The Citadel Military Academy. First-year cadets — knobs as they were called because their shaved heads resembled doorknobs — underwent their initial year of training at Arsenal before completing their studies at The Citadel, the overarching entity, which had considerably more space.

On December 20, 1860, South Carolina formally seceded from the Union. In organizing its military units a month later to prepare for war, the South Carolina General Assembly combined the Corps of Cadets at The Citadel and Arsenal into the Battalion of State Cadets and designated the two institutions as The South Carolina Military Academy.

Marshall had finished his third year at the academy on April 8, 1861. As his family lived in Charleston, he was asked to remain at school for several more days to be of assistance to some of his instructors. Many faculty members — with the threat of war looming overhead — had left the institution for the field to prepare for the potential hostilities.

On the afternoon of April 11, a small boat embellished with a white flag pushed off from the tip of the peninsula surrounding the city of Charleston. The vessel carried three envoys representing the

Confederate States' government, established in Montgomery, Alabama, two months before.

Slaves rowed the men more than three miles across the harbor to the hulking Fort Sumter, where U.S. Army Lieutenant Jefferson C. Davis — no relation to the newly elected president of the Confederacy Jefferson Finis Davis — met the arriving delegation. The lieutenant led the envoys to Major Robert Anderson, the fort's commander, who had been holed up with a garrison of eighty-seven officers and enlisted men since Christmas. They were the last symbol of federal power in South Carolina, a state known for its fervent secessionist stance.

Even though Anderson and his men had been offered safe passage from the island, he refused to yield the Union stronghold. At four-thirty a.m. on April 12, Confederate troops fired on the fort.

Upon hearing the news, numerous Citadel cadets who'd already left for home returned to the academy. They were ordered to White Point Gardens and then attached to various military units manning the harbor and assigned to take charge of the five-, six- and twelve-pound cannons located at the furthest east promenade of the battery.

Gunfire was exchanged between the opposing forces for thirty-four hours until the outmanned Union side was forced to surrender. With the declaration of war, many cadets left both Arsenal and The Citadel to join the war.

In June of 1862, cadets of both academies formed a cavalry unit known as the Cadet Rangers. Having graduated by then, Marshall joined the unit at the rank of second lieutenant. The Cadet Rangers became part of the 6th Regiment, South Carolina Cavalry, and were assigned to train the regiment's officers and non-commissioned officers.

The Rangers, Marshall included, took part in several engagements along the South Carolina coast before the majority of the young soldiers were deployed to Virginia in the early months of 1864.

With the death or wounding of key Confederate officers, a select group of Cadet Rangers was promoted one rank and sent to train regiments in other areas of the South that lacked skilled military leaders.

Marshall was chosen to travel west to train troops under the command of Lieutenant General William J. Hardee, stationed in northern Georgia. The Confederate Army was preparing for the advance on their position by troops under the command of William Tecumseh Sherman, who had been promoted to the rank of major general by Ulysses S. Grant. Grant himself had recently advanced to the highest rank in the Union Army — general-in-chief — after his performance in the Battle of Shiloh, where he'd been wounded in the hand and the shoulder and had three horses shot out from under him.

When he wasn't putting men through their paces, Marshall was assigned patrol duty. It was a mundane task, but meeting Miss Rose this afternoon certainly enlivened his route for the day. His regiment was scheduled to be in Dallas for another six days or so. *That would be just enough time to get better acquainted with the young lady.*

War or not, he imagined it was still polite to follow proper protocol if a young man was interested in courting a young woman. He'd need to get permission from her father if he wanted to spend some of his off-duty hours with her.

Never one to spend too much time wrestling over a decision, Marshall immediately turned his horse back in the direction of the dry goods shop. He'd keep an eye out from the end of the block and watch Miss Rose as she made her journey back to her house. When he had some free time this week, he'd return to her place and formally introduce himself to Mr. and Mrs. Rose.

Having been entranced by the golden undertones of the young lady's skin, he was curious to see if she got her looks from her mother or her father. He'd find out soon enough.

Chapter III

Alice was nearly giddy. She'd actually pulled it off.

The princess endearment had thrown her for a moment, but it appeared to have been an attempt on the young man's part to woo her. He couldn't possibly know anything of her background.

After assuring herself that First Lieutenant Kent had gone on his way, she'd slipped back out of the dry goods shop and set off on foot to the house with the green rose bush planted in its backyard.

Briefly removing her gloves, she observed her hands. While her palms were so light that they could have easily passed as white, the unblemished honey-colored skin on the other side of her hands attested to her true heritage.

She'd had the opportunity to lighten her face this morning with rice powder "borrowed" from her half-sister Susanna. At fifteen years old, the ingénue was already working on perfecting her skills for attracting beaus. And she had all the necessary *accoutrements* to do so.

Seeing as young men were few and far between at this stage of the war, Alice doubted that the girl would have any need to make up her face anytime soon. She'd slip the powderpuff back into the drawer of the dressing table before Susanna would be any the wiser.

The fact that the first lieutenant didn't question her further was evidence that Alice could actually pass for white. As proud as she was of her royal African heritage, it was necessary to downplay that in order to accomplish the mission on which she was embarking.

Pulling the gloves back on, Alice quickened her step and turned right to enter the alleyway. Stopping alongside the treasured bush, she reached down to run one of the petals between her fingers. Bringing herself to full height, she smoothed her skirt and strode to the back door of the house. She gave the doorframe a solid rap with her knuckles and then stepped back.

The sound of shuffling footsteps came to her ears. A moment later, the lace curtain covering the window adjacent to the doorway was pulled back. Alice saw someone eying her through the glass. The curtain dropped back into place, and the door was cracked open.

"May I help you?" asked the petite, fair-skinned woman, peeking around the corner of the door jamb.

Alice quickly sized the lady up. She was elderly, perhaps in her late sixties. The sage-colored dress she wore was made with homespun fabric, devoid of any lace or trimmings. Its style was reminiscent of frocks popular earlier in the century. Pinned to the shoulders of the dress was a plain shawl, the points of which hung down over its bodice. Atop her greying hair was a white linen cap covered by a black coal-scuttle bonnet.

The epitome of a true Quaker female. She was a Plain Friend as opposed to a Gay Friend who would have been clothed in much livelier colors.

"Ma'am," said Alice politely, "I'm inquiring if you'll be accepting any packages soon."

The woman stepped outside the door and glanced from left to right. With no one in hearing distance, she replied, "Accommodations can be made for next Tuesday. How many should I expect?"

Relief coursing through her, Alice quickly

responded, “Three full-sized and two petite ones.”

“That’s acceptable. However, all shipments must leave the premises within twenty-four hours.”

Alice nodded in agreement. It was just as well anyhow. The less time holed up in Dallas, the better. A person didn’t want to wear out their welcome or cause any harm to befall a newly found “friend.”

“I shall see you Tuesday after sundown, ma’am.”

“Yes. Please make the delivery to the root cellar. The entrance is on the far side of this building.”

After thanking the Quaker woman, Alice left the property and scurried back to the dry goods shop. On the way, she gave praise to the good Lord and Saint Mary, the Blessed Mother. All those weeks on her knees, praying the Rosary, had paid off. She was being shown the path for her family’s freedom.

At the shop, Alice ticked off the list of goods to the shopkeeper that Mrs. Williams had asked her to pick up. It had been several weeks since she’d been at the establishment. While the gentleman piled items on the wooden counter, she meandered through the space, perusing various items for sale. It was enjoyable to imagine having the wherewithal to purchase something brand new. She ran her fingers over a piece of butternut calico fabric that would make a fine dress. *Someday...*

All merchandise accounted for, everything was wrapped up in butcher paper and tied together with a length of string. No money was exchanged as the order was put on the plantation’s bill as usual. After saying good day, Alice slipped out the door.

The business people in town had always been cordial enough to her, particularly if they knew the Williams family, but she had no regrets leaving this locale behind her. She looked forward to the time when she could start her life fresh on equal footing with any other citizen of the United States.

Those reveries kept her going as she fought through the struggles of her day-to-day existence. Things were bound to get more difficult before they got better, she realized. But, if they could all make their way to safety, the trials and travails would be worth it.

With the package on the gig floor, Alice untied the horse from the hitching post and, reins in hand, settled onto the seat.

"Ya," she commanded, causing the horse to pull away from the sidewalk.

As she drove back to the Williams' plantation, she went through her plan for the upcoming flight step-by-step. Everything must be timed precisely, or their lives would be endangered.

The items they'd need for the trip were stashed inside a one-room cabin on the edge of the estate. For the last month, she and Josiah had shared the space with Marcus, his woman Daisy and their baby Abraham. *Soon enough, I'll have to stop referring to him as Baby Abraham.* At six months, he seemed like a giant next to Josiah, who was only a month-and-a-half old.

Alice enumerated the items on her list for what felt like the hundredth time. There were rags to deaden the sound of the wagon wheels, twine to affix the cloth in place, a bit of face powder in a glass jar, a dozen boiled eggs and two loaves of bread that she would abscond from the pantry in the big house, cloth for diapers and two receiving blankets.

While it wasn't a necessity, she would also be bringing something along that was of great sentimental value to her. The tortoise shell grooming set — which included a comb and handheld looking glass — was her most treasured possession. She wasn't a person to admire herself in a mirror, but it was one of the few gifts that she'd ever received in her life. And the only one from her mother who'd been gone some six months now.

Waves of pain washed over her as she thought about that saintly woman. Despite all that she'd been subjected to in her life, Célia Williams carried herself with stately pride. Regardless of her mistreatment, she'd never spoken poorly of anyone. Every pain that she suffered was offered up for another hurting soul.

In some ways, Alice felt responsible for her mother's death. She could never forget the sorrow in the woman's eyes when she learned of her daughter's condition. Witnessing another generation undergo what she'd endured during her thirty years working in the big house was too much for her heart to bear. One day that overworked organ just gave out.

In actuality, it would have been unlikely that Célia — or Cecilia as the Williams family called her, preferring the Anglicized pronunciation of the name — hadn't been aware that the younger master of the plantation had been taking advantage of her daughter.

When Alice found herself with child, she'd done everything that she could to keep her condition a secret as long as possible. Eventually, the day came when her apron no longer hid the bulge under her smock, and she was forced to confess the situation to her mother.

She'd dreaded the conversation, not sure how the

woman would respond. The evening that she'd approached her mother, who'd finally had a chance to put her feet up after a long day attending to her mistress' countless needs, Alice felt tongue-tied, which was unusual for her. Doing her best to skirt around the unpleasant details, Alice admitted that she was in trouble.

While her mother didn't blame her for what happened, the expression in her eyes was like a dagger to her heart.

As fearsome as that ordeal had been, it paled in comparison to what she may be facing in the coming week.

Chapter IV

He kept far enough back so that Miss Rose wouldn't hear the sound of the hooves striking the ground. As the horse trod along, Marshall glanced at the wooded areas on either side of the road. The terrain reminded him of the forests near Charleston, where he had played as a youth.

An only child, Edwin Marshall Kent II was the apple of his mother's eye, his father's pride and joy, and a welcome issue for his parents who had thought that they were barren. Like John the Baptist's parents, Elizabeth and Zechariah, the couple was blessed with a pregnancy in their twilight years. Both were approaching forty the day that Marshall — as they chose to call him to differentiate him from his father — came roaring into their lives.

Hearing the wail that he'd made when the midwife tapped his behind upon his entry into the world should have warned his parents that their child would have a zest for living,

According to his mother — the estimable Mrs. Clara Marie Kent – from the get-go, Marshall had been on the move nonstop. Even as an infant, he was said to slow down just long enough to nurse and immediately afterward squirmed his way out of his mama's arms.

Appropriately, the woman was named after a saint — Saint Clare of Assisi — certainly it took the patience of a holy woman to raise such a spirited boy as himself. He enjoyed setting out on escapades, exploring and climbing. He had his share of bumps, bruises and broken bones through the years to prove it.

Marshall lived life with gusto. He enjoyed being the center of attention in his group of friends, the same fellows with whom he'd chummed ever since he could remember. Their families attended St. Mary of the Annunciation on Hasell Street in Charleston together.

While some Protestant denominations had private schools, there were no Catholic schools nor private boarding schools in the city when he was growing up. Thus, the boys were enrolled together at the Charleston public elementary school nearest their parish. It was one of five public schools in the municipality.

When state schools had first opened at the turn of the nineteenth century, the law allowed any white child to attend the free schools, with preference given to poor families. The institutions were dismal, to say the least. Most working families were too proud to send their children to what was termed a "pauper school" and the upper and middle classes — which included the majority of families in the low country where Charleston was situated — chose to have their children taught at home.

Only a small percentage of children actually attended school in one-room schoolhouses. But, when they did, their attendance was spotty as they were expected to help their parents run their farms or bring in wages, as meager as they were for children.

The school system was overhauled the year that Marshall and his buddies started school. In the 1840s, the idea was introduced to use local property taxes to pay for public education. The notion gained steam when they were in secondary school because of a landmark educational experiment in Charleston.

The renowned educator C.G. Memminger, who'd been one of their teachers, set about establishing a true public-school system in their city. Drawing on the best models of schools in the north, Memminger installed a modern curriculum and hired skilled teachers and administrators at his school. Through his efforts, families of all classes were attracted to the system.

That one school paved the way for the modern education system adopted by the whole state. The key to Memminger's success had been using the local tax base to fund the school and ridding the school of its pauper image.

No child under eight was admitted to his school unless they had some proficiency in reading, so Marshall and his friends all had a bit of education under their belts by the time they entered first grade. The curriculum was expanded as they progressed in their studies. Subjects taught in school included spelling, reading, writing, arithmetic, multiplication tables, parsing — the study of parts of speech and sentence components — geology and grammar.

There was a particular emphasis on penmanship, with contests held each year to determine which students showed the highest proficiency in that field. While Marshall's writing was legible, he didn't care to put in the time to make it commendable.

In the warm-weather months, students attended school in the morning from eight until noon and then three until five o'clock in the afternoon. In the fall and winter, school started an hour later in the morning, but they still had two hours off in the middle of the day to go home for lunch. School was in session year-round with just one two-week break for Christmas and another two-week break for Whitsuntide, the week beginning with the seventh Sunday after Easter.

Marshall was coddled at home by his mother, but his schoolmasters showed him no leniency. The slightest infraction could bring a rap across his knuckles from the instructor's ruler. There was no use complaining to his father about the unfairness of it all. Edwin Marshall Kent lived by the axiom, "Spare the rod, spoil the child." At least in theory – he never actually used corporal punishment on his own son.

It didn't take long for Marshall to learn to toe the line at school. Curtailing his mischievous behavior was worth the effort to avoid getting punished.

He could still feel the stinging sensation from the teachers' rulers. Marshall cracked his knuckles to push the memory back into the recesses of his brain. His mind swiftly reverted to the present time.

After a good twenty-minute journey from town, Miss Rose made a right turn onto a paved lane, lined on either side with pecan trees, which led up to a stately plantation. A sign with the words Pecan Hall arched over the entrance to the property.

Her father must have done well for himself. *Guess I'll need to be on my best behavior when I make his acquaintance.* It was time to shine up the old-school manners that had been beaten into him. He wouldn't have admitted it when he was a youth, but that discipline had probably been worth it. It certainly prepared him for his time at The Citadel. And, it could very well pay off in this present time as well.

Marshall took one last glance as the gig drew closer

to the house. Now that he knew where the young lady lived, he tugged Maximus' reins to turn him around. He had to take one last sweep through Dallas before his shift ended.

Headed back in the proper direction, he happened to see an ebony-skinned man walking on the opposite side of the road. Assuming that he belonged to the plantation, Marshall hailed him, hoping to get some information about the master of the house.

"Excuse me," he said, slipping off the back of the horse.

Seeing the uniform, the man looked at him leerily.

"Yassuh," he replied, dropping his gaze.

"Do you live at that plantation up ahead?"

"Yassuh. Just coming in from the back fields."

"Excellent. I've plans to return this evening to speak with the owner. I would imagine you know him?"

"I knows who he is but can't say he knows me."

"May I ask what Mr. Rose's first name is? And how he prefers to be addressed? Perhaps he's a doctor or a military man?"

The man's brown eyes swung up, and he stared directly at Marshall.

"Don't know no Mr. Rose."

Marshall was taken aback. *How could he not know Miss Rose's father? Didn't he just say that he knew the owner of the plantation?*

"Maybe I'm a bit confused. Isn't your master's surname Rose?"

The man shook his head.

"Who owns this plantation then?"

"That'd be Massuh Williams, sir."

Williams? Was the girl trying to deceive him? Did she purposely give him a false name? Perhaps there was more to Miss Rose — or whatever her name was — than met the eye. Now he was really intrigued.

Chapter V

With the horse and gig being attended to by a groomsman, Alice carried the package into the summer kitchen adjacent to the big house and set it on the table. Two female slaves were busy preparing the Williams' family supper.

The building was set back from the living quarters. With fire always being a threat, it would be infinitely better to lose the small structure than the whole house. Alice had always found comfort spending time there. With its large fireplace and stone bake oven, it was warm and welcoming.

As a child growing up in the big house, she'd enjoyed visiting the ladies who worked in the kitchen, peering up at them over the large rough-hewn wooden table, and watching them as they chopped vegetables or kneaded dough. If the bread was ready, more often than not, she'd be gifted with the heel of the loaf.

Even though the Williams family proper disdained the end pieces, that was her favorite part of the loaf, especially fresh out of the oven, slathered with freshly churned butter. It melted the second it came into contact with the warm bread.

The family didn't know what they were missing. It was the same with brisket. That meat from the lower chest of the steer was a tough cut and, consequently, the only part of the animal that the whites deemed worthy of giving the help to consume. What they didn't realize was that the slaves cooked the meat using West African methods and that the toughness was counteracted with long, slow cooking. When the abundance of connective tissue broke down, it gelatinized into a rich and tender slab of meat.

Alice's mouth watered just thinking about it. There wouldn't be a lot of things that she'd miss once she left the big house, but the food and meals that she shared with the staff would always be a treasured memory. She couldn't fathom ever eating anything as delicious as the fare that they prepared, as meager as their portions were at times.

Of course, she'd miss her people too. She couldn't care less if she ever laid eyes on another Williams in her life, but the African folk — especially the ones running the house — were some of the kindest and most inspiring human beings that she'd ever met.

It pained her to think that she was leaving and couldn't say goodbye to anyone. She wanted to tell her friends how much they'd meant to her, especially in the dark days of the past year with the pregnancy and the loss of her mother.

If she could, Alice would wander through the entire three-story house to relive the memories of her years living there. Even though her fellow workers were enslaved, they managed to create some moments of joy in their lives. They were grateful for even the smallest of things.

While it wouldn't be prudent to step into the big house and stir up any suspicion, there was no harm in walking through the space in her mind. Alice took a seat on the bench adjacent to the far wall of the kitchen and recalled each room, one by one.

Viewing the house from the front walk, the double doors opened to display the two-story entryway. It was a grand sight — for visitors, at least. The help tasked with climbing the ladder to light the candles in the candelabra each night would have been more than happy to settle for a less-spectacular entrance.

To the right was the formal parlor, which was reserved for distinguished guests and local dignitaries. With its fancy wallpaper shipped across the ocean from England, the velvet-tufted mahogany Chippendale furniture and ornate fireplace flanked by an intricately carved mantle, it was quite opulent. The settee and armchairs were upholstered in shades of red and purple, the color of royalty.

The Williams family considered themselves upper crust, though there was no evidence as far as she knew that they really were.

Wouldn't that be something if they found out that they had been in the presence of royalty all these years and never realized it? Alice could just picture their mouths agape when they were presented with that tidbit of information.

Mrs. William's side of the family was of the Maryland English and one of the original founders in 1792 of The Church of the Purification of the Blessed Virgin Mary in Dallas. The English had the church to themselves until families fleeing the French Revolution arrived in Georgia. Then the French slave-holding families came from Haiti — including Mr. Williams' parents — after the Slave Revolt in 1798.

It was said that Mr. Williams' grandfather had been murdered during the uprising in Haiti. The assailant had been executed but, in the years since, the story had been embellished to the point that a hatred had festered in the Williams' family for all Negroes. Of course, that distaste hadn't stopped them from replenishing their stock of African slaves after they immigrated to America.

And it certainly didn't stop them from fraternizing with Negro women, thought Alice bitterly. Of course, if those encounters hadn't happened, then her mother would never have been conceived, nor herself, nor sweet and innocent Josiah. Which goes to prove that every cloud has a silver lining. Or, most every cloud. It was a stretch finding the good in some of the things that had transpired on this plantation.

Mr. and Mrs. Williams were church-going people. They'd actually met each other at The Church of the Purification of the Blessed Virgin Mary and had been sweethearts since their grammar school years.

It never ceased to amaze Alice how people, who put on such a righteous façade when they were fraternizing with fellow congregants after Mass, could be such different people behind closed doors.

What happened to the "Love thy neighbor as thyself" sentiment that the priest talked of at Mass on Sundays? Alice may have had to stand at the back of the church with the other household help, but she'd heard those words as loud and clear as the rest of the congregation.

While Mrs. Williams wasn't cruel to the house slaves, she certainly made it known that she was superior to them. If they didn't do her bidding promptly or as specified, she had no qualms about sending them outside for a "word" with the overseer. As long as she didn't witness the punishment that he meted out, it apparently didn't bother her conscience.

Mr. Williams, on the other hand, wasn't averse to

doling out a whipping where he saw fit. As a matter of fact, he seemed to find some pleasure in it. He had a fierce temper, and God help anyone who vexed him, white or black. While he didn't dare outright attack a fellow Caucasian, he had means of exacting his revenge on them six ways from Sunday.

Alice shook, just thinking about the man. After what he'd put her mother through, she couldn't even stand to look at him. When he'd passed away last year, she'd felt nothing but a sense of relief.

Returning to her mental walk through the big house, the next room was Mr. Williams's study to the left of the foyer. The door was always closed. Few people other than himself and business associates ever spent time in there. Even after his death, the help was only allowed inside to dust or pull up the rugs to beat on the clothesline.

Beyond that room was the formal library, filled floor to ceiling with books on every topic that a person could imagine. Susanna and Stewart – who was two years her senior – were the only legitimate Williams' children. They showed scant interest in the space, but the room called to Alice every time that she passed by. She could borrow as many books from there as she cared to, as long as they were neatly shelved when she finished reading them.

At the back of the house sat the dining room with a table large enough to accommodate sixteen diners. The family ate every meal there, and it was the spot where they hosted dinner parties. Adjacent to that was the butler's pantry and a smaller kitchen where the food was plated before serving.

Tucked into the rear corner of the house was the

lavatory with its washtub, a commode to conceal the chamber pot and a dry sink. Of course, only the immediate family members were allowed to use those facilities.

The help shared an outhouse a hundred yards away from the main house, well out of sight of the living quarters. While it wasn't necessarily convenient, at least it was only used by a handful of people. The accommodations for the slave cabins were much more crowded.

There were six bedrooms on the second floor of the big house. Mr. and Mrs. Williams each had their own sleeping chamber; there was a room for Stewart, one for Susanna and two spare bedrooms for company. A shiver of fright went through Alice as she thought about the young master's room. That was one memory that she hoped would fade in time.

Open space on the third floor housed all the female help. Marriage amongst slaves was illegal, but even if the women did manage to jump the broom with their loved one, they were still expected to reside in the big house so they could be at the beck and call of Mrs. Williams. It was hard to imagine how any of them ever came to be with child, considering how little time they got to spend with their husbands.

Wedded or not, Mr. Williams had always encouraged his slaves to procreate. While childbirth did take women away from their work for a week or two, it was worth the inconvenience. Slave children created a continual stream of income for the plantation. The owners could either expand their operations with a new generation of workers or fatten their bank accounts by selling the offspring on the open market when they were of age.

The children of the house slaves were allowed to live in the big house until they were six years old. In that timeframe, they were educated to a degree and trained to work, following in the footsteps of their parents, learning their trades through observation and imitation.

There were two schools of thought amongst the plantation owners when it came to educating Negroes. Some of the men feared that giving slaves educational opportunities was a dangerous proposition because it lessened their effectiveness as workers. Other men opined that slaves were more valuable if they could read and write. Mr. Williams happened to be in the latter camp.

For the most part, black folks who'd been offered the chance to get schooling eagerly took advantage of it. Some were able to hire themselves out to work in town. The bulk of their pay was handed over to their owners each week, but they did get to keep a portion. Through time, some slaves saved enough to buy their freedom.

Slaves with the ability to write were able to break the evening curfews for Negroes. They would present permits — allegedly signed by their owners — to be out and about unescorted. Since so few police officers could read themselves, the public servants were easy enough to deceive.

A number of Southern whites were of the conviction that it was impossible to cultivate the minds of slaves without arousing in them a spirit of self-assertion, in essence, rebellion. Consequently, a law was passed in 1843 forbidding the education of Negroes.

Despite the warning that any white person who was

convicted of teaching a slave to read or write would be subjected to a fine of up to one hundred dollars or six months imprisonment, financially, it had still been a sound investment for Mr. Williams to have his slaves receive a rudimentary education. They fetched a higher sum at the slave market, so it was a calculated risk.

The education of most of the Negro children in the house ended once they learned the fundamentals of reading and writing. Even if their mothers were more highly educated, they dared not instruct their children. The punishment for a Negro teaching another Negro was even more severe than a white person teaching a Negro. They could be subjected to a whipping — not exceeding fifty lashes — and a fine. Informers were entitled to half of the bounty, which enticed people to become snitches, even against their own brethren.

The Williams' bastard children, including Alice, were educated by a governess alongside their half-siblings and were allowed to continue their schooling through the secondary grades.

Célia, who'd come from a long line of educated African women, passed along her love of learning to Alice, whose inquisitiveness knew no boundaries. Through the course of the years, the young girl had read every book in the Williams' library at least once. She was particularly drawn to tomes on science, geography, history and anatomy and aspired to put that learning to good use someday. It appeared that the time might be arriving sooner than she'd anticipated.

Chapter VI

Marshall mulled over the information that he'd received from the man. This Miss Rose harbored a secret. Of course, he'd realized that the moment that he'd laid eyes on her. She may have done a plausible job disguising herself, but he ascertained quickly enough that she was of African heritage.

Whether she was a mulatto, quadroon or octoroon was hard to tell as her face was powdered, and she'd been wearing gloves. Half, quarter or an eighth African, it was all the same. If she was attempting to hide her identity, then she was up to something.

While a lot of folks in this neck of the woods would take issue with that subterfuge, it didn't concern him. He knew that life wasn't easy for Negroes in America. Heck, if he'd been held as a slave in a foreign country, he'd have done everything in his power to escape too.

His father ran an import business in Charleston and had several free blacks in his employ working on the docks. Helping out there on summer breaks during his years at The Citadel, he'd labored side by side with those men and got to know some of them rather well. For the most part, they were a good lot. He considered a couple of the fellows around his age to be friends.

Chatting with them on work breaks, it seemed as though they had the same hopes and aspirations that he and his white friends had. They wanted to find that special someone to marry someday, put a roof over their heads, start a family, and provide for their children a life better than what they'd experienced.

Despite the fact that Marshall graduated from The Citadel, he wasn't square in the successionists' camp. He did not support slavery in any shape or form. Like the majority of Southerners, his family didn't own slaves.

From his perspective, the war between the states wasn't to protect the institution of slavery. The educated people with whom he'd conversed favored a gradual emancipation of the slaves. If this happened over the course of, say, five years, it would allow the economy in the South to adjust to a paid labor system without suffering an economic collapse.

As much as Marshall relished adventure, in reality, he'd found no excitement in the prospect of going to war. Truth be told, if the threat of hostilities hadn't been looming over America's head, he'd have never given attending a military academy a thought. In his younger years, he'd had every intention of enrolling at the College of Charleston.

Founded in 1770, it was the oldest educational institution south of Virginia and the thirteenth oldest in the United States. The school became the nation's first municipal college in 1837 when the city of Charleston assumed responsibility for its support. Money from the city was used to enlarge the main academic building, to build a lodge and to fence in the core of the campus, Cistern yard.

Had Marshall attended school there, it certainly would have saved the Kent family a good deal of money. He could have resided at his father's house instead of on campus. On top of that, the tuition would have been considerably less than The Citadel, which set the elder Kent back some two hundred dollars a year — a small fortune — seeing as his son was a "pay cadet" rather than a "beneficiary cadet."

The regulations adopted by the Board of Visitors for the military academy specified that there was to be an equal number of pay cadets and beneficiary cadets.

Regardless of how their fees were covered, young men were chosen from South Carolina's twenty-nine judicial districts based on their moral character, academic qualifications and fitness for military service.

Seeing the writing on the wall concerning the war, his father — unceasingly loyal to the Palmetto State — set his mind on having his only child attend a military academy and graduate as an officer and not have to enlist as an infantryman. He'd considered West Point Military Academy for Marshall since its student body consisted of young men from both the North and the South but dismissed that idea as the campus was located in enemy territory, the state of New York. So, The Citadel it was.

Once his father had his mind made up, there was no changing it. The onus was placed on Marshall to make himself an acceptable candidate. Thanks to his mother — who had been charged with his religious formation through the years and made sure that he received all his sacraments — he was about as up-to-speed in the morality column as any boy his age.

As far as his bodily fitness went, Marshall was in good form. He was athletically inclined. That being the case, he desired to be at his peak physically before his admission interview, so he set out a game plan of daily calisthenics to do just that.

Academics, on the other hand, was a different issue.

School came easy for him, but the amount of work it took to earn above-average grades versus average grades had never been worth it for him. His ultimate goal had been to graduate high school, not reign at the top of his class.

Once it was made known to him how competitive it was to get into The Citadel — and what the stakes were for not getting into a military academy — he upped his game. Marshall spent the last two years of secondary school bulking up his grades and his body. By the time he graduated, he was a specimen of a young man and, consequently, received that coveted appointment.

It was gratifying to have earned placement through his own endeavors. Knowing his father, the man would have pulled whatever strings were necessary to get his offspring into that renowned school. From Marshall's perspective, being handed a spot that a student more deserving should have gotten was akin to stealing. He'd have enlisted before doing that to someone.

While it was a relief to have his place at the school, he'd had misgivings as he stepped on the campus of The Citadel as a fourth classman. Not only was this education costing his father an arm and a leg, but the rigors he faced as an incoming cadet were nothing short of intimidating.

Attending the College of Charleston would have been an enjoyable endeavor, with days a blend of schooling and more enjoyable pursuits. While females weren't allowed to attend the college, they were permitted to fraternize with the male students. The campus hosted various social events throughout the year where the sexes were allowed to comingle.

Sounded like the ideal institute of higher learning to

Marshall. A pristine campus with the right mix of studies and fun. Somewhere to while away four years of his life before he had to join his father in the import business, learning the intricacies of running the enterprise so he could take it over someday.

His plan had been to major in business. That sounded like the path of least resistance to obtaining a degree. He had pictured himself enjoying campus life rather than spending all his time with his nose stuck in dusty old schoolbooks.

The Citadel was the polar opposite of a community college. Marshall's first few weeks there were rocky, to say the least. Like the rest of the cadets, he was worked so hard that he had no time for fun — or mischief for that matter, even if he'd had the mind to make some.

When authorities said that the academy had a reputation for academic standards and strict military discipline, they weren't jesting. Apparently, they'd adopted many of the regulations — as far as discipline and training went — from West Point's playbook.

Academically, The Citadel developed a curriculum that differed from their rival's. A plus in Marshall's opinion, the Board of Visitors endeavored to provide the cadets with as broad of an education as possible — both scientific and practical — to prepare them for leadership roles beyond the military service.

During their four years of study, cadets undertook a rigorous course of academic studies in addition to their military training and their duties around the campus. This course of instruction included Modern History, Geography, English Grammar, Algebra, Geometry, Descriptive Geometry, Trigonometry, French, Bookkeeping, Rhetoric, Moral and Natural

Philosophy, Architecture, Civil and Military Engineering, the Science of War, Topographical Drawing, Chemistry, Physics, Geology, Mineralogy, Botany, Constitutional Law, and the Laws of Nations.

In addition, cadets were schooled in the military arts, including Artillery, Evolutions of the Line, and Duties of Non-Commissioned and Commissioned Officers.

Initially, Marshall balked at the course load, the training, the marching, and the physical fitness regimen but, within weeks, he began to relish the challenge and faced each day with a determination to succeed.

Life as a cadet at The Citadel was demanding. They were awoken each day at the crack of dawn, and it was a good sixteen hours before the young men's heads hit their pillows again. School days were spent in class, doing drills and performing their assigned duties. They had an infantry drill or military drill each weekday. Evenings were devoted to studying.

On Saturdays, they had room inspection and inspection under arms. Church attendance on Sundays was mandatory. As a child, Marshall had not enjoyed going to church, being forced to sit still under his father's watchful eye and enduring what seemed like endless sermons from their priest. Surprisingly enough, once he was in military school, church became the highlight of his week.

It was two hours of tranquility, introspection and a respite from being ordered around. He began to listen closer to the homilies and internalize the message. He prayed with reverence rather than by rote as he had in his youth.

He was permitted to leave the campus for an hour every Saturday to go to Confession. At first, it was an excuse to get some time away from the institution, but soon enough, it became a beloved routine for him. Marshall couldn't believe that so few other cadets took advantage of the opportunity. It was hard to imagine walking around weeks or months on end with sins weighing down a person's soul. He felt like a new man every time he stepped out of the confessional.

As there were no athletic pastimes on campus, Marshall found an outlet for his competitive nature. He joined a debate team. As he hailed from the Low Country, he became a member of The Calliopean Society. They went head-to-head against The Polytechnic Society, which drew its members from upstate South Carolina.

The debates were spirited, or — as most of the debaters admitted — acrimonious, particularly when the topic centered on politics or war. One of the highest honors at the academy was to be elected president of one of the societies, a position reserved for a member of the first class. Marshall considered running for that position in the fall of 1862 but didn't think the accolade justified the amount of time and energy that he'd need to expend to achieve that rank.

During his time on the debate team, he learned the skills suited for a legal professional. That caused him to change his major from business to law with the thought of opening his own practice when the hostilities came to an end.

As much as he savored life in South Carolina, the state was getting too populated for his taste. With his never-ending craving for adventure, he set his eyes on staking a claim in Texas. Who knew? He may be the first attorney to hang his shingle in that untamed land.

In the meantime, he meant to put his lawyerly investigation expertise to work and do some digging on Miss Rose. At the first available opportunity, he would make his way back to the Williams' plantation to pay her a visit.

Chapter VII

Alice followed the dirt path to Marcus' cabin. He and Daisy were in from the fields for the day. As she walked through the door, Miss Dolly was just handing Abraham to his mother. A hacking cough welled up from the little one's chest. *That's concerning.*

The lady patted Abraham on the head in a soothing manner and then scooped Josiah off the sleeping mat and lovingly placed him in Alice's arms. Holding the baby close, she snuggled her nose into his neck and inhaled his sweet infant scent. Everything she was plotting to do was for him. Even if she died trying, she was going to see that he found his way to freedom.

Josiah slept soundly as she gazed at his face. If a person saw the stick-straight mop of dark brown hair atop his head, his hazel eyes and fair skin, they may not even realize that she and him were related. But his long black eyelashes, pronounced cheekbones and the fullness of his lips were a testament that they came from the same stock.

As Miss Dolly made her goodbyes, Alice went up to her, wrapped her free arm around the woman's shoulders and gave her an affectionate squeeze. The woman stopped in her tracks and looked at her questioningly. It was out of character for her to go around hugging people, but she couldn't help herself.

Feeling a bit awkward, Alice stepped back.

"I just want to thank you, Miss Dolly," she said sincerely. "I can't tell you what a help you've been. Not only to me but to all the women on this plantation."

"It's been my pleasure, Alice," the woman replied.

"You take care of yourself, hear me?"

"Yes, ma'am."

"I'll see you first thing tomorrow morning. And every morning after that."

"Yes, ma'am," she replied, keeping her eyes downcast so the woman wouldn't see the dishonesty in them.

She watched as Miss Dolly retreated from the cabin and shuffled off toward her own abode. Although she'd never gone through childbirth herself, the elderly woman had been by the side of every female slave who'd given birth on the plantation since she'd arrived as a teenager fresh from Africa. It was said that her father was a shaman in her home country of Tanzania.

Shamanism was a religious practice, and its practitioner, the shaman, was believed to interact with the spirit world while in a trance. The goal was to direct spiritual energies into the physical world for healing or other purposes. Regardless of the fact that Miss Dolly was a female, folks considered her to be a shaman and treated her with the respect accorded to that position.

For Alice, as a lifelong Catholic, Shamanism sounded like voodoo — which also happened to be practiced by a handful of slaves who'd come to the plantation via Trinidad. The thought of either spooked her. Thankfully, Miss Dolly seemed to use whatever power she had for good, rather than trying to rain misfortune upon — or exact revenge on — her fellow human beings.

With her rheumatism, the aged woman could no longer work in the fields. As she was too old to put on the sale block, Mr. Williams had allowed her to remain on the plantation to take care of the slave children until they were old enough to join their parents working the fields. The woman had an inborn maternal instinct and treated every child under her care as if he or she was her own.

She'd been a godsend to many a woman on the plantation, including Alice. It pained her to leave any of her people behind, but getting her immediate family out of the clutches of Mr. Williams' cruel son and his overseers was her primary mission.

Glancing down at Josiah again, she marveled at what a miracle it was that he'd survived. If it had been up to Stewart, she would have never had a chance to hold him in her arms. Once that ogre knew that she was expecting, he insisted that the child be eliminated.

She couldn't do it. Her baby was as much a child of God as anyone who resided on the grounds of Pecan Hall, and he deserved to live and be raised by his mother.

Some slaves on the plantation were allowed to exist as a family unit, with a husband, wife and children all living under one roof.

Other families were split up, with the father and mother being owned by neighboring masters. They called those relationships "abroad marriages" and, even if the couple did not live together, the men were allowed to walk several miles to the neighboring plantation to visit his family on Wednesday and Saturday nights if his obligations to his master had been fulfilled.

Free labor for the production of wealth lay at the heart of slavery. As long as the goods — be it cotton, tobacco, corn or rice — kept coming, people in both the South and the North chose to turn a blind eye as to how those products made it to their doorsteps.

Slaves worked from early morning until late at night. Women had just a few days off after delivering a baby and then were expected back in the fields; the only allowance was extra breaks for them to nurse their infants. Most large plantations had a woman like Miss Dolly to take care of the little ones.

By the time a child turned eight, they were expected to be working, whether that was watching after the owner's youngsters, running errands, fanning flies from the owner's dining table, or taking lunch pails to the owners' children who attended school. Eventually, they worked the fields alongside their parents.

The slave quarters' yards served as the center for interaction between enslaved family members. When they were out of eyesight and earshot from their owners, overseers and patrollers, they had the latitude to host celebrations or prayer meetings. House slaves like Alice were instructed in the Catholic faith and accompanied the Williams' family to Mass.

Enslaved women cooked meals in their cabin fireplaces and sewed, mended or quilted late into the night. In what little spare time they had, the men fished or hunted, sometimes taking their sons along, to supplement the somewhat meager food rations.

Like other plantation owners, Mr. Williams debated on the advisability of keeping slave families intact versus splitting families up. It appeared that keeping families together made it less likely that a man or woman would run away. Consequently, some owners encouraged "marriage," thus the practice of "jumping the broom" as a ritual symbolizing marriage amongst the slaves. Some magnanimous owners had even been known to give a small gift or two for the "newly-wedded" couple.

That didn't necessarily mean that owners allowed men and women to make their own choices when it came time to pick a mate. As in selecting a stud and a mare for ideal breeding purposes, some owners paired up men and women essentially for the same end, with no concern as to whether that couple had feelings for each other or not.

The threat of families being separated continually hung over the slaves' heads. Great sorrow ran through the plantation when an impending sale approached. Negroes were considered a commodity and were purchased or sold as finances warranted. A slave could be sold to liquidate assets to pay off debts as part of an estate when their owner died, or they could be shipped off if they were considered to be a troublemaker.

Families could be split as part of an inheritance when their owner passed away, or they could be divided and gifted to newlywed white couples who were starting out on their own. It was said that one-third of children lived in a situation without a father, a mother or neither.

Some slave owners purposely separated slave children from their parents to decrease the development of affection between them. That was the case in Alice's family. She was the third generation of slaves to live in the big house at Pecan Hall. Of all the children born into their family in that time, only one child in each generation was selected to live with its mother and reside alongside the Williams' children.

That golden child was always a female, hand-picked by the master of the house at the time. The youngsters who didn't make the grade were either relegated to the cabins to be raised by other Negro families or sold.

In some respects, Alice should have felt fortunate to have been considered the cream of the crop by the elder Master Williams and allowed to live in the big house. Her life was relatively easy compared to what the children experienced who lived in the shacks and worked the fields.

That privilege also brought with it a sense of guilt. Her two younger sisters and her little brother had been sold after the youngest had been weaned. Her mother's heart broke when her children were ripped from her arms.

Since that day, Alice had tried to prove her worth. She was advanced in intelligence and worked hard at her studies. Master Williams often commented on her ability to read and recite, trotting her out to perform for his dinner guests as though she were a trained monkey.

As uncomfortable as it made her feel, her owner also took pride in her remarkable looks, especially when he mentioned something in front of his own Susanna, who was somewhat plain. He couldn't get over how Alice's unblemished skin glowed. Her high cheekbones, full lips and straight, pearl-like teeth made her a rare find in his eyes.

According to him, a person would be hard-pressed to find a white woman who matched her attractiveness. Between that, her intelligence and how learned she was, she was quite the treasure.

He often compared her to an Egyptian princess. Not that he actually knew any. Even though he had hundreds of books in his library, Alice seriously doubted that he'd read any of them. Perhaps he could name Cleopatra, the most famous royal Egyptian woman, but she didn't imagine he'd know who Twosret, Hatshepsut, Nefertiti, Merneith or Sobekneferu were.

It couldn't be said that he wasn't proud of Alice and how she turned out. More likely, though, he was proud of himself for producing such a specimen. He was her father, after all.

Chapter VIII

The afternoon and early evening dragged on. Marshall went through the motions of inspecting troops, handing out discipline for minor infractions and filling out the never-ending paperwork for his superiors. While his mind had continually wandered back to Pecan Hall and its beautiful occupant, he'd been kept busy sunrise to sunset for the last several days. Today he would finally finish early enough to make a visit to the plantation.

To get his thoughts off Miss Rose until his assigned duties were complete, he stepped back in time, recalling the years that proceeded his fateful assignment in northern Georgia that allowed him to meet that lovely young lady.

Marshall enrolled at The Citadel as a fourth-class cadet in the fall of 1858. With war brewing, officers and cadets were called upon to perform military duties. A laboratory on the campus was utilized for the manufacture of ammunition.

On December 20, 1860, two years into his studies, South Carolina seceded from the Union. Even though both Arsenal and The Citadel still functioned as military academies, from that point on, classes were interrupted periodically when the governor called the cadets up for military service. They were assigned tasks that included manning the heavy guns, performing guard duty, and — Marshall's preferred duty — escorting prisoners.

He didn't see the men as enemies but considered

them fellow human beings who just happened to have a different point of view than his own. Truthfully, he enjoyed conversing with them and learning about their home lives, the schooling they had, and what they'd done for a living prior to their military service.

There was no need to mistreat them. Marshall was always armed, so no one was going anywhere. He tried to imagine himself in their shoes. If he'd have been a prisoner, how would he have wanted to be treated? His mama had instilled the Golden Rule into him as a child, and it stuck.

Once the war was in full swing, for the most part, the cadets were insulated from the hostilities. That was, until a beloved instructor was lost on the battlefield. Charleston native Charles Courtenay Tew taught at Arsenal the year that Marshall was a fourth-class cadet. The man was not only in the initial graduating class of The Citadel in 1846, he was also the first honor graduate from the school.

Tew had been an instructor at his alma mater after graduation, then took a year off to travel across Europe to study military tactics. Upon his return, he was designated Commandant of Cadets and, in 1857, was appointed superintendent of Arsenal Academy.

When North Carolina seceded from the Union, Tew was one of the first two colonels of the Confederate forces appointed by Governor John Ellis. He was commissioned to the 2nd North Carolina State Troops under the command of Brigadier General George B. Anderson of the Army of Northern Virginia. During his fourth campaign, on the eve of his promotion to brigadier general, September 17, 1862, Tew was killed in action at the Battle of Antietam while leading his regiment.

Marshall thought of the man often when he and his fellow cadets were training green recruits in newly formed military units. The instructors traveled as far as Virginia to work with troops on the frontlines.

Eventually, the war came to their own doorstep. Officers and cadets at The Citadel actively participated in a number of engagements and campaigns in defense of Charleston and South Carolina as a whole.

In addition to their attack on the *Star of the West*, there was Wappoo Cut in November of 1861 and the James Island skirmish in June of 1862, shortly after Marshall's class graduated.

They'd also been tasked with defending the city from July to October of 1863, but, by that time, he'd been assigned to train troops throughout the South that were on the leading front of the war.

It'd been two years since Marshall had laid eyes on the Corps of Cadets flag that went with them into each battle, but he could picture it like he'd seen it yesterday. The flag was composed of a field of blue Lyons silk. One side displayed the arms of the state of South Carolina and the name "South Carolina Military Academy" with the date 1857, in memory of the day that the flag had been presented to the corp — February 22, 1857 — on the occasion of Washington Light Infantry's semi-centennial celebration in Charleston. On the other side of the flag was stitched an elaborate wreath of oak leaves, surrounding the inscription "Fort Moultrie, Cowpens, King's Mountain, Eutaw Springs," and below that, "Our Heritage."

As he thought of that flag, he happened to spot a different flag on a side street in Dallas. The *Stars and*

Bars — the first national flag of the Confederacy — was prominently displayed on a building in front of him. With its circle of thirteen stars — representing the southern states of North Carolina, South Carolina, Mississippi, Florida, Alabama, Georgia, Louisiana, Texas, Virginia, Arkansas, Tennessee, Missouri and Kentucky — in the navy-blue canton with its two red stripes and one white stripe, it resembled the flag of the United States.

Marshall could see why it'd been replaced last year with the *Stainless Banner*. The Confederate Congress had specified that the new design be a white field with the union to be a square of two-thirds the width of the flag, having the background red: thereupon a broad saltire of blue, bordered with white and emblazoned with mullets, or five-pointed stars, one for each of the Confederate states.

With the economy being what it was, it was understandable that the homeowner hadn't upgraded to the newer design. By this time next year, it could already be redesigned. It seemed to be an annual occurrence.

Finishing up the last of his correspondence for the day, Marshall shoved all the leftover sheets of paper into his desk drawer to give the room a semblance of organization and extinguished the two-wick lamp. It was fueled with camphene, a mixture of one part turpentine, four parts alcohol and a touch of camphor oil extracted from the wood of camphor trees, and emitted a pleasant aroma.

The lamp had burners with long wick tubes set at angles to burn separately, a design meant to lessen the risk of explosion. The flames were extinguished by placing metal caps over the tubes, which was safer than blowing them out. As much as he dreaded paperwork, he wasn't of the mind to incinerate his office to eliminate it.

That done, he stepped out of the small room, closed the door behind him and headed to the stables to get Maximus from his stall. The horse had been with him since he'd enlisted in the Cadet Rangers. Its Latin name had originally been bestowed on successful military commanders but, in time, became a common first name, borne by several of the Church's early saints.

The combination of military prowess and defender of the faith suited the animal well. With its pedigree and royal bearing, a colloquial name such as Buddy would not have been acceptable. Knowing the horse as he did, the beast wouldn't have answered to anything below his station anyhow.

When the horse was saddled, Marshall left the compound and trotted off in the direction of Pecan Hall. As he neared the outskirts of the town, he saw a wagon a ways off approaching town. He immediately tugged on the reins to get the horse to turn onto a side street.

Marshall had no idea who was in the vehicle but, as it was his duty to patrol the area, he felt that he needed to err on the side of caution and keep an eye on it just to make sure the occupant was in town for a legitimate reason.

Passing the first house on the street, Marshall pulled his horse into the space between the structure and the next building to stay out of view of the passing conveyance. He tied the horse to a bush and peered around the corner of the house and waited for his target to get closer.

The vehicle quietly rolled past the spot where he was hiding. It took everything for Marshall to keep his jaw from hitting the ground. The profile of the driver was unmistakable. *What in tarnation is Miss Rose doing back in town again?*

Chapter IX

Time crawled by until it was finally Tuesday evening, and they were able to make their escape. Seeing the town come into view, Alice sighed in relief. She and her companions had made it safely through the first leg of their journey.

That sense of respite was short-lived, though, as a lone rider approached them from the west. Thankfully, a moment later, the man turned down another street and went south.

She could never remember being so jittery in her entire life. Of course, she had just cause considering the precious cargo laying on the floor of the vehicle. Marcus and Daisy, each holding one of the babies, were concealed under a pile of quilts.

Thanks to a thimbleful of whiskey, the children slept soundly, quiet as mice. It pained her to drug them, but one cry would be all it took to draw notice to themselves.

Alice had gone back and forth on whether or not to include Marcus and his family in her escape plans, but ultimately, for their safety, it seemed the prudent thing to do. Though the two of them weren't biologically related, it was common knowledge on the plantation that Marcus considered her to be his younger sister. If she was found missing, the first person that the overseers would interrogate would be him.

The day that her own brother and sisters were sold, Alice had fallen into such a state of despair that her mother feared that she might give up on living. As young as she was then, she knew that Gabrielle and Juliette — or Gabby and Julie as the master called them — and little Jacques were going away forever, not just on a visit to distant relatives on another plantation as some people tried to convince her.

Jacques was such a sweet little fellow. She'd taken care of him since he was born as though he'd been her own baby. His cherubic smile lit up the room, and when he giggled, a soul couldn't help but join along.

He was so adorable, even the white folks admired him—particularly Master Williams' sister. When Jacques was a toddler, she was smitten with him to the point that she asked her brother to give the youngster to her and her new husband as a wedding gift.

As appalling as it was, the man had actually granted the woman's wish. Being the shrewd businessman that he was, he worked out a deal with his new brother-in-law that the three siblings were a package deal. While Jacques — or Jackie as the bride had dubbed him — was a present, Gabby and Julie would be sold at fair market value.

With the deal struck, the two girls and the little boy were bundled up and sent off to Rosewood Plantation to await the new couple when they returned from their honeymoon tour of Europe.

Alice trembled. Come hell or high water, someday the four of them would be reunited. Gabrielle, named after the archangel Gabriel, whose name meant "God is my strength," was going on fifteen. Alice prayed that the war would end and all slaves would be freed before she turned sixteen. As she very well knew, there was no joy in coming of age for a Negro female.

Juliette — whose name, appropriately enough,

meant youth, beautiful and vivacious — would be thirteen now. Jacques was ten. Rosewood Plantation wasn't that far from Pecan Hall, but it may as well have been a thousand miles away as Alice was never allowed to visit there or have any contact with her siblings.

Her despair had known no bounds. Who could say what would have happened if Marcus hadn't stepped in at that time to watch over her and take on the role of older brother in her life?

In reality, Marcus was actually more like a father to her than a brother. When he'd discovered what happened to Alice at the hands of the master's son, he vowed he'd break that scoundrel's neck with his bare hands. It took three men to hold him back from searching out Stewart at that very moment.

Alice had begged him to leave things be and not get involved in the situation, but Marcus had blood in his eyes from that point on whenever he saw the younger Master Williams on the grounds. His fury boiled beneath the surface of his skin, and she worried that someday it would bubble over, and she wouldn't be able to constrain him.

Marcus didn't have the schooling and religious training that she had, but he certainly knew the story of Jesus Christ. That man, the son of God, was horribly persecuted yet still forgave his betrayers before he died.

No matter what injustices had been inflicted on Marcus, he handled it in the meek and subservient manner in which he'd been trained to respond to authority figures. Alice knew the real him, though, and he wasn't who he appeared to be to the overseers, whose bravery was fortified by the whips and pistols that they brandished. Those cowards weren't half the man that her adopted brother was.

Alice glanced over her shoulder to make sure the passengers were still hidden. It had been quite the undertaking getting them off the plantation. They'd had to wait until it was pitch dark, then she and Marcus snuck off to where the horse and wagon were secured. They tied the rags around the wheels, loaded the vehicle, and then went back for Daisy and the babies. Rolling away from the plantation grounds, Alice had taken one last look at the buildings and fields behind her.

As unfortunate as the circumstances of her youth were, everything that had happened in her life had formed her into the young woman that she was now. Someday, when this was all behind her, Alice would do whatever it took to find forgiveness in her heart for her persecutors and then go to Confession to seek forgiveness for her wrongdoings as well.

Jesus' words as he hung on the cross came to her. "Forgive them, for they know not what they do." Was it possible that the plantation owners were so enmeshed in the institution of slavery, similar to the feudal system that had existed in Europe for centuries, that they didn't recognize the barbarity of their way of life?

Of course, that didn't give them license to be cruel, either physically or mentally. In certain respects, Alice had been fortunate. With her status in the big house as the master's progeny, no one dared lay a hand on her. Even Stewart knew better than to mar his cherished prize.

The thought of that sinister young man chilled Alice

to the bone. It would be evil to want a human being to suffer eternal damnation, but if she ever wished that upon anyone, it would be Stewart. Lord only knows when she'd finally be able to erase his image from her mind.

Chapter X

Once the wagon had passed him, Marshall thought it wiser to follow Miss Rose on foot to avoid being detected. He left his horse tethered to a bush and walked through the yards tracing the young lady's path.

A few blocks further west, she turned the horse down a residential street, traveled another several blocks and then cut off into an alley. At the pace she was going, it was easy enough to keep her in sight.

The second building in, she pulled over, sprung off the seat and then proceeded to secure the horse to the hitching post. She scurried to the far side of the house. A minute later, she reappeared.

Reaching into the back of the vehicle, Miss Rose pulled some quilts aside and grabbed a package. Hugging it close to her chest, she stepped back, and a beast of a man unfolded himself from the floor of the vehicle. He grabbed another package and then held a hand out to assist a young woman to the ground.

While Miss Rose had been able to disguise herself when they'd first met, there was no hiding the heritage of the other two. In the darkness of the night, all that Marshall could clearly make out were the whites of their eyes.

He stood stock-still, watching the male and female Negroes distance themselves from the conveyance. The man handed his package to the younger woman and protectively placed his hand on the hollow of her back and escorted her behind Miss Rose. They retreated to the spot that she had come from just moments before.

Muffled coughing came to his ears. He strained to listen closer. The woman accompanying the oversized male turned to glance behind her. The shifting clouds allowed a sliver of moonlight to illuminate the yard. It was then that Marshall realized that – rather than packages – the bundles that the two women carried were swaddled infants.

His heart constricted in his chest. As a commissioned officer in the Confederate Army assigned in northern Georgia, one of his duties was to keep an eye out for fugitive slaves. *If that bunch isn't attempting an escape, I'll eat my hat.*

Having spoken with Miss Rose face to face, he was in a quandary. It was one thing spying on a nameless stranger, but it was an entirely different thing surveilling someone he actually knew. It made her a very real person, regardless of what Article One, Section Two of the Constitution of the United States declared.

That ruling stated that any enslaved individual would be counted as three-fifths of a free person for the purpose of determining congressional representation. The Three-Fifths Clause didn't allow slaves to vote but did increase the political power of the slaveholding states, including his home state of South Carolina.

Focusing his eyes on the retreating Miss Rose, he couldn't help but reflect on how enticing she was. It wasn't just her striking looks. From their brief interaction, he'd sensed that she was intelligent, sharp-witted and wise beyond her years.

He didn't imagine her to be the kind of person to put other human beings' lives in jeopardy on a whim. If she was helping those folks escape, there had to be a compelling reason to do so, which would explain why she had misled him when they first met.

A dutiful Confederate officer would immediately confront the group. Which was exactly what he should be doing, considering his position. Admittedly, he wasn't like most of the other men of his rank and standing. Regardless of how he'd been trained, Marshall had a difficult time considering any human being less than another.

He felt that each individual was a unique creature made in the image and likeness of God. Not to say that there weren't some bad apples, but for the most part, the humans that he'd met in his lifetime were decent people. All in all, there were probably only about a dozen rotten folks in the world. They just got around a lot.

Regardless, there was no rush to do anything at this moment anyhow. He'd hold back and watch the scene unfold to get a better handle on the situation before he stepped into the quagmire.

Marshall made his way to the opposite side of the property to see if he could watch their activities from another angle where he'd be less likely to be discovered. Seeing no one in the front yard, he snuck under the open windows and made his way to the far corner of the building.

Poking his head around the edge, he saw the door of the storm cellar cracked open. His eyes strained in the dim light. Would there be any more activity, or had they sequestered themselves under the house for the night?

He'd give it a few minutes. Meanwhile, he needed to consider his options. Not doing anything could be considered an act of treason on his part. Marshall recalled the oath that he'd made to the Confederate Army when he joined the Cadet Rangers.

"I, Edwin Marshall Kent II, do solemnly swear that I will support and defend the Constitution of The Confederate States against all enemies, foreign and domestic; that I will bear true faith and allegiance to the same; and that I will obey the orders of the President of the Confederate States, Jefferson Davis, or his successor, and the orders of the officers appointed over me, according to regulations and the Uniform Code of Military Justice."

Heck, he could even remember the preamble to the Constitution of the Confederate States. "We, the people of the Confederate States, each State acting in its sovereign and independent character, in order to form a more perfect union, establish justice, insure domestic tranquility, and secure the blessings of liberty to ourselves and our posterity, invoking the favor and guidance of Almighty God to ordain and establish this Constitution for the Confederate States of America."

It was similar enough to the preamble to the Constitution of the United States that it hadn't been that difficult to memorize. The seven articles of the Confederate Constitution? Now, that was a different story.

Technically, slaves were the property of the plantation owners. Would it be breaking his oath if he didn't return those fugitives to where they belonged?

One tenet of the constitution popped into his memory banks. "No slave or other person held to service or labor in any state or territory of the Confederate States, under the laws thereof, escaping or lawfully carried into another, shall, in consequence of any law or regulation therein, be discharged from such service or labor; but shall be delivered up on claim of the party to whom such slave belongs, or to whom such service or labor may be due."

Didn't get much clearer than that. But truthfully, wasn't his first priority to God? What was that Gospel passage that talked about rendering unto Caesar the things that are Caesar's and to God the things that are God's? Were slaves actually property to be held by humans, or were they the property of God? In his heart, Marshall knew the answer and needed to act accordingly.

In time, Miss Rose reappeared from the shadow of the building. As she untied the horse, he quietly slipped through the grass, hoping the pounding of his heart wouldn't give him away as he drew near.

Busy unlooping the reins from the hitching post, she never heard him come up behind her.

He clasped her elbow in his grip. "Miss Rose..." he said, the words barely a whisper.

She whipped around, reins dangling from her ungloved fingertips, a look of fear in her eyes.

"We need to talk."

Chapter XI

She'd nearly jumped out of her skin when that iron-clad hand ensnared her elbow. Her knees slightly buckled in relief when she saw who had her in his grasp. Praise God, it was First Lieutenant Kent. Any other man, and she feared that she'd have been pistol-whipped on the spot.

Instinctively she knew that he was different from other men. She'd looked into his eyes when they'd first met and saw only sincerity in them. So different than the other white men she knew.

Alice prayed that he was just checking up on her welfare, seeing as it was so late at night. Her mind raced through a number of lies that she could present to him. A sick friend who needed company? A visit to the parish to pray in front of the Blessed Sacrament?

Either would work. Giving the man a broad smile, she put on her best southern airs.

"Oh, my goodness," she gushed in a fine Georgian drawl, "if it isn't First Lieutenant Marshall Kent. You nearly scared the living daylights out of me."

His eyes locked on hers. While she normally was adept at reading people, his façade at the moment was impenetrable.

"Gracious me, but you're a strong one," she continued, batting her long, dark eyelashes at him. "But you can unhand me. Rest assured, as startled as I was, I have no plans to swoon."

He didn't flinch.

Getting desperate, Alice resorted to another angle. "First Lieutenant, if you'd kindly loosen your grip, I'd appreciate that. You wouldn't want me to be sporting a bruise tomorrow, now would you?"

Nothing. *Rats.*

Switching tactics, she put on an offended demeanor. "I do swear, sir, if you don't release my arm this very instant, I may need to scream. The neighbors might come to the conclusion that you've put me in a compromising position."

"That would be tragic, Miss *Rose*," he replied in a saccharine tone. "Pardon me for being less than gentle with you. I'm used to disciplining my men. As you can imagine, I'm not wont to treat them with kid gloves."

The thought of being disciplined by a man as tall and muscle-bound as the first lieutenant was alarming, to say the least. He even made Stewart Williams appear to be a weakling.

Moments later, he released his grip on her, much to Alice's relief, but she was less than assured when he repositioned his hand on the holster encasing his revolver. She'd no need of face powder; her face undoubtedly turned three shades whiter when she saw the gun, moonlight glinting off the polished wooden grip. *How many men has he put into the ground with that weapon thus far in his career?* She didn't want the recognition of being the first woman felled by his shot.

"Let's take a walk to that copse of trees over yonder, where we can chat in private for a moment, shall we," the man said solicitously, guiding her across the street as protectively as a beau would escort his sweetheart.

Stiffening at his touch on her upper arm, Alice did as

he suggested, all the while scanning the scene in front of her, searching for an escape route. Being just six weeks post-partum, she wasn't in tip-top sprinting shape, but considering that her life may be on the line, she'd give it her all.

The chances of fleeing became slimmer once they made their way through the patch of eastern white pines. Coming to an abrupt halt, the man immediately encircled her with his arms, trapping her against the trunk of a tree.

"Is that really necessary, First Lieutenant?" she demanded, squirming to put space between herself and the soldier.

"I'd say it is, miss," he said, drawing closer. "This actually serves two purposes." A grin came to his face, revealing teeth that were just as straight and white as her own. She couldn't tear her eyes away from his visage.

"It will prevent you from fleeing. And, should anyone happen upon us, they will assume that we're star-crossed lovers sneaking out from under your father's watchful eyes for a tryst."

A gasp escaped from Alice's lips. And it wasn't a feigned one either. *How dare he!* If she'd been able to get a hand free, she'd have slapped him across the face for his impudence.

"Well, I've never...." Her voice trailed off when he moved in ever closer.

"I'm not so sure of that, Miss... what did you say your name was again?"

"Rose," she spat out, trying to recall if a white lie was considered a venial sin.

"Ah, yes, Miss *Rose*. It's a lovely surname and, by

chance, the ideal topic to begin our little tete-a-tete."

She tilted her head and looked at him leerily.

"I know that isn't your surname. For some reason, you've chosen to initiate our relationship being less than truthful with me."

Relationship? Her first thought. *How in the world does he know that?* came directly after.

"What is your name? Your full name, first and last?"

Initially, Alice said nothing until the soldier pressed himself closer to her body.

"We can do this the easy way or the hard way."

Instinctively, a word tumbled, "Alais," she said, emphasizing the French pronunciation. It was her baptismal name, so no mistruth there.

"Alais," he repeated, matching the pronunciation. "Like Alice?"

Letting out a sigh, she mumbled a reply. "Close enough."

"See, that wasn't so difficult, now was it, Alice?"

She bit her lip in consternation.

"Now, let's get to the surname."

That was more complicated. Technically, she had no surname. But somehow, he'd found out that her last name wasn't Rose. Had the first lieutenant followed her back to the plantation? She could kick herself for not being more cautious when she'd returned from town the day that they'd met.

If she claimed the Williams name for her own, maybe he'd think she was a true daughter to Mr. and Mrs. Williams.

With no other idea surfacing, she answered evenly. "Williams."

"Atta, girl."

Was he mocking me? Alice gritted her teeth together and waited to see in which direction the line of questioning would go.

"Miss Alice Williams." The words rolled off his tongue. In general, she preferred the French pronunciation of her name, but the American version sounded just fine in his distinct Southern accent.

"What brings you out on such a fine night as this?"

Alice shifted her eyes downward, and she considered how to answer him. He'd seen her by the wagon, but how much more had he witnessed?

She hesitated to answer. The soldier pulled one hand back and used the tip of his pointer finger to gently tilt her head up so that she was staring directly into his eyes.

"Hasn't your mama ever told you that it's better to tell the truth than get caught in a lie?"

Mechanically, she nodded.

"Trust me; things will go much better if you're straightforward with me."

Alice nodded again, keeping her eyes engaged with his. She searched the depths of them and, seeing no malice, began to feel that she may be able to trust him. Heaving a sigh, she blurted out, "I was helping someone."

A tear threatened to escape from her lower eyelashes. She pursed her lips in frustration. There was nothing worse in her mind than showing weakness. Alice blinked hard.

Lieutenant Kent brushed the tear away with his thumb. This time the smile he gave her was sincere. "Maybe I can help too."

Chapter XII

Marshall stood still as Alice surveyed him up and down. *Assessing my character, perhaps?* He released her from his grasp, took a step back and pulled himself to his full height so she could complete her evaluation.

She appeared satisfied with what she saw, so he picked up from where he'd left off.

"From what I could see, it appears that you've transported two blacks, a male and a female, and two infants into town."

Reluctantly, Alice gave a slight nod.

"May I assume that family came from the Williams' plantation?"

"You may."

"And may I also assume that the help you're offering them is to escape the bondage of their master?"

Alice stood mute.

"Remember, I said I could help. But I won't be able to do anything unless you give me the whole story."

With a look of resignation, Alice answered. "Your assumption is true."

"What would make you do that?" he asked. Before she could answer, a thought dawned on him. She must be a free black. That would give her the latitude to travel into town unescorted.

The woman hesitated, appearing as if she sought the appropriate answer.

"Are they under the threat of peril?" Marshall offered.

"They are, sir."

"I can see that you're hesitant to go into full detail, and I can understand why, considering that I'm bedecked in the Confederate gray. However, I'd ask you to consider not judging this book by its cover."

She didn't seem to know how to take his request.

He continued. "Putting two and two together, I have concluded — and correct me if I'm wrong — that the family you've accompanied into town has an immediate need to vacate Pecan Hall. They must be dear to you for you to put yourself in such danger to get them off the plantation."

Hearing no dissent, he plowed forward. "I gather that the house across the street is considered a safe house, perhaps part of what I've heard called the Underground Railroad?"

Now Marshall was starting to feel some unease about the situation himself. He may have accidentally stirred up a hornet's nest. Was this young lady a so-called conductor for that organization? Perhaps this wasn't her first go-round.

Regardless, Pecan Hall wasn't more than three miles from town. When it was discovered that slaves were missing, the bloodhounds would be set loose.

The house standing there — secure as it allegedly was — didn't give them nearly enough distance from the trackers. As much as he didn't want to get entangled in the girl's situation, he had empathy for that family and those twin babies, even if he hadn't seen them up close. He didn't want their capture and punishment to be on his conscience. It was imperative to get them further out of harm's way.

"Alice, I would imagine this house was just a

temporary stop, is that correct?"

"Yes, First Lieutenant."

"If we're going to be working together, you may call me by my first name."

"Yes, sir," she replied automatically. Then her head shot up. "Working together?" She gazed at him quizzically.

"That's what I said." He gave her a reassuring smile. "Do you know the location of the next house to which they were to travel?"

"Yes, it's outside of town, heading west. The idea is to throw the slave catchers off by going that direction instead of north, which is the most common route to freedom."

This little lady *does* have a good head on her shoulders.

"Is there anything that would prevent you from sending those folks there a day ahead of time?"

"There could be an issue with that," admitted Alice. "The owner of that house isn't a Quaker. As a matter of fact," she hesitated, "he isn't even an abolitionist."

"And yet he offers his property as a stop on the escape route?"

"Well, I wouldn't exactly say he's offered it up."

Marshall looked at her closely. "Expound on that thought, if you please."

"Packages are only delivered there when the gentleman is out of town."

"Is he the type of man who travels much?"

"I'd say so," she replied.

"And to where might this man be traveling?"

"If I were to guess, I would say to Richmond."

"As in Richmond, Virginia?"

Alice nodded, and Marshall's stomach dropped.

"As in the capital of the Confederacy?"

"Yes, sir."

"Are you telling me that someone who works for President Jefferson Davis has had his house overrun by travelers on the Underground Railroad?"

"I wouldn't go as far to say his whole house. Just the root cellar."

Marshall sighed. "Okay, we've gotten this far. Whose house is it?"

"It's the McGinnis house."

"As in the John Thaddeus McGinnis house? Secretary of the Interior of the Confederate States of America John Thaddeus McGinnis?"

She nodded again.

Time was a-wasting; he'd have to make a quick decision on how to proceed. *A person who enjoys adventure lives for these moments, don't they?*

He mentally ran through several options and then verbalized his plan.

"Who knows when the missing slaves will be noticed, Alice. Let's get them out of the root cellar and back into the wagon. I'll escort you to the McGinnis home, and — with the hope that the distinguished Mr. McGinnis is not on the premises — we'll deposit them safely there and get you back to the plantation."

A stricken expression came to Alice's face. "That's not possible."

"Why not?"

Taking a deep breath, Alice replied. "I cannot go back there. I must accompany the others."

"Why on earth would you do that?"

"Because it's my fault that they're in this predicament."

Chapter XIII

As the horse and rider accompanied the wagon out of town, silence hung between her and Marshall. He hadn't been able to disguise the look of surprise on his face when she'd made her proclamation. Notwithstanding, he was still with her, so he couldn't have taken the news too poorly.

Alice tried to figure the man out. He was a Confederate soldier and, in that capacity, he most certainly would have been justified marching her off to the jailhouse rather than traveling with her to the McGinnis property. He hadn't, though. That didn't make sense.

Every so often, she surreptitiously glanced in his direction and shook her head in wonder. What would cause him to go against the dictates of his commander in chief and help abscond with property that belonged to a citizen of the Confederacy of the United States?

She'd never met a male of such character before. Certainly, there'd been men of her acquaintance who attended Mass every Sunday. From all appearances, they were as pious as saints. But that was pure showmanship. That piety was put on like wearing their Sunday best once a week for the benefit of the congregants of The Church of the Purification of the Blessed Virgin Mary. Once they were out of view of the parish, they resumed their wrongful ways. *Just like the Pharisees back in Jesus' day.*

After she and Marshall cleared the town limits, Alice could no longer hold back her curiosity. This would be the last time that she'd ever see First Lieutenant Kent. She was keen to find out what made him tick, somewhat how a scientist studies a creature to which he had never been exposed before.

"First Lieutenant?"

He cocked his head and raised an eyebrow at her.

"Pardon me... Marshall."

The young man nodded approvingly.

"May I say on behalf of myself and my fellow... travelers that we are profoundly grateful for your assistance."

"It's my pleasure."

His broad smile threatened to melt the wall of ice that Alice had built around her heart. She had to quell the urge to put her hand to her chest to see if something physiologically was occurring inside her. That idea was preposterous, of course, so she kept both hands on the reins.

She had never in her life exposed her heart to any man, and she certainly wasn't going to start with a Caucasian. A Confederate soldier at that. Alice pinched the skin above her inner wrist to bring her mind back into focus.

"Marshall, seeing as we'll be parting ways after we get to the McGinnis house, I thought maybe we could talk for a few minutes and learn a bit more about each other."

Or, as the plan was laid out in her mind, she'd be asking all the questions, and he'd be doing all the answering.

Apparently, the young man was amenable to that proposition as his smile deepened. *Oh, my goodness, that cleft in his chin, how did I miss that before?* She sat straighter on the seat of the conveyance in an attempt to get her train of thought back on track.

The effort was pointless. A combination of handsome looks and a sincere and kind nature was too much for any female to withstand. *Good Lord, I'm as addled as a schoolgirl. Thankfully, we'll only be together for a short time, or I could fall for this man. What would maman say?*

Truth be told, probably not much other than telling her daughter that it'd be a good idea to listen to her heart for once, rather than analyzing everything half to death. Regardless of how that woman had been treated by the men in her life, her mother didn't judge people. She said that job was reserved for the good Lord.

Another one of *maman's* sayings came to mind. "Hurting people hurt." But, try as she might, Alice couldn't envision what hurts Master Williams and his son could have experienced in their lives that could come anywhere near the pain that they inflicted on their slaves. Or, truth be told, their own blood relatives.

With their time together dwindling, she commenced her cross-examination.

"From whence do you hail, Marshall?"

"The great state of South Carolina, Charleston to be exact."

"Can you tell me about your family?"

"Not much to tell. It's just me, my mama, Clara Johnson Kent, and my father, Edwin Marshall Kent I. I was a late-in-life surprise for them, so I don't have any brothers or sisters."

"I see," said Alice. "Then Marshall is a nickname?"

"It's the only name I've ever been called. My mother

called me that since I was born. She said one Edwin in the house was enough."

"Your parents are still alive then, I take it?"

"That they are. My father runs an import business in Charleston. Of course, business has been spotty as of late. The Union set up a blockade of Charleston Harbor as part of their strategy to defeat the Confederacy. Their intent was to cut the Confederate states off from the rest of the country. And the rest of the world, for that matter."

Alice was engaged in his dissertation, enthralled by his baritone voice.

"The Union blockade extended some thirty-five hundred miles along the Atlantic and Gulf of Mexico coastlines and the lower Mississippi River. Fortunately, we've got competent men captaining the blockade runners. For the most part, those steamships have been able to break through the barriers. Even so, traffic at the docks has decreased substantially since I left home."

"I can imagine," Alice noted. "Has it been a while since you've seen your parents?" As far as she was concerned, this conversation could go on forever. His voice was mesmerizing and, unlike her, he enjoyed being in the limelight.

Marshall rolled his eyes up to the left as he calculated. "Well, let's see. I graduated from The Citadel in the spring of '62, joined up with the Cadet Corp a month later. Seems to me, the last time I laid eyes on them was after the battle of James Island before I shipped out to Virginia to start training new recruits. That'd make it... twenty-three months."

The Citadel? Alice's eyes opened wide. That was one

of the most prestigious military academies in the United States. Good looking, a gentle spirit and a keen mind? *Now that is a winning combination if I've ever heard of one.*

Earning a spot in a military academy was no easy task. She'd witnessed the process. Stewart Williams had applied to the Georgia Military Institute and been turned down flat. Even his father couldn't bribe his wayward son in. The young man had the brains but was sadly lacking in moral aptitude.

"Your *maman* must miss you something fierce," Alice said.

"You can say that again. She was always fussing over me when I was a youth. But, according to the letters I've gotten here and there, she's redirected her energies to the Ladies' Aid Society in Charleston. They collect food, clothing, medicine and anything else usable for the troops. I figure by now Mama's knit enough socks to stretch from Charleston all the way to Spartanburg."

A smile came to Alice's lips. It'd been a long time since she'd heard anything amusing. She couldn't remember the last time she'd laughed. Being with Marshall was good for her soul.

"Miss Alice, I feel like I've been monopolizing this conversation," admitted the soldier. "What about you? You have a mamma and a pappa and maybe a couple sisters just as pretty as you?"

A blush came to Alice's cheeks. Partly because of his words of flattery and partly because she was uncomfortable with the question. What answer would satisfy his curiosity yet not give away too many incriminating details about herself? Her gut told her that he could be trusted, but the uniform made her want to err on the side of caution.

"My mother passed away earlier this year."

"I'm so sorry to hear that." Marshall leaned over from his saddle and patted her arm. "I would imagine she was quite the woman to have raised such a stellar daughter as you."

A lump formed in Alice's throat. She hadn't allowed herself time to grieve after her mother's passing. Rather, she'd put all her energy into formulating an escape plan. *There will be time to mourn down the road,* she'd reminded herself.

Swallowing hard, an answer rolled from her lips. "She was the most incredible human being I've ever known. My advanced education, my catechism, my knowledge of the world, can all be attributed to her efforts in my formation."

Marshall gave Alice's arm a light squeeze and encouraged her to continue. "You have other family still, I hope."

That question presented a quandary. If Marshall took her bait, then he would be under the impression that she was one of the legitimate Williams' children. If she answered truthfully, her real identity would be revealed.

There was a chance that he was helping her because he thought she was an abolitionist with a kind heart and zealous enough to help some poor Negro family escape from bondage. If he knew the truth, would he march the lot of them back to Dallas?

It wasn't worth the risk. She opted to be truthful but vague.

"Oh, yes. We're quite close."

Alice furtively slid her eyes to the back of the wagon and the mound of quilts.

"I'd love to hear about them."

"And I'd love to tell you all about them, Marshall, but wouldn't you know it, there's the McGinnis house up ahead. We'll resume this conversation another time."

Chapter XIV

Marshall wasn't sure what to make of that comment. Some other time? Was she implying that they would somehow be seeing each other again? *Does she know something that I don't know? Or is she being facetious?*

Dismissing the thought, he let out a sigh and dismounted from his horse. Grabbing the reins of both animals, he led them to a wooded area off the road so the sound of the wagon wouldn't awaken members of the McGinnis household.

That done, he turned to help Alice step down from the conveyance. Encircling her waist with his hands, he lifted her up slightly and then gently set her on the ground, his hold on her lingering a bit longer than necessary.

The situation between the two of them caused him to wonder. He knew that God had a plan for every one of His children, but if this young lady wasn't meant to be in his life, why had the Good Lord deigned to have them encounter each other? Was it just a coincidence?

Is there really such as thing as a coincidence? He really didn't reckon that there was. God brings people into other people's lives for a reason. *And for some reason, I was meant to meet Alice.*

But why her and why now? His plan had always been to find a girl to settle down with after he'd finished school and seen some of the world. The war had actually given him the chance to visit numerous states that he'd never seen before. Maybe it provided him the opportunity to find a wife as well.

Marshall had always felt that he'd been born under a lucky star. Even with a civil war ravaging their country, he'd had the good fortune to receive training from one of the top military academies in the nation and come out of school as a commissioned officer. With his rank and his innate leadership ability, he had his choice of assignments upon graduation. He'd been an attractive commodity to the higher-ups.

Now with things well in hand in Dallas, he was to report to Little Rock, Arkansas next. Camp Nelson, just outside the city, had been hit by an epidemic of measles and typhoid fever during the fall of 1862. In a two-month period, nearly fifteen-hundred Arkansas and Texas soldiers died of one or another of the diseases. The deceased had been buried in unmarked graves in the surrounding hills.

Unfortunately, the commander after whom the camp had been named — Brigadier General Allison Nelson, who led the 10th Texas Infantry Regiment — succumbed to typhus himself in October of that year.

After Nelson's death, the 10th Texas joined up with the 4th Brigade of Walker's Texas Division under Major General John George Walker. For a year, Walker had solicited volunteers to join the depleted regiment. When that didn't work, he resorted to conscripting recruits against their will. Men between the ages of eighteen and thirty-five were rounded up — many from ranches and farms in the western territories — and shipped back east for training.

That's where Marshall stepped in. He had a knack for taking green "volunteers" and turning them into fighting men. While he was generally known for his easy-going demeanor, he could crack down on subordinates when the need arose. He learned that from the best — his upperclassmen at The Citadel.

Marshall's thoughts went back to the black man that he'd just helped disembark from the conveyance. He watched as the giant slipped into the root cellar of the McGinnis house with his lady and their children. Perhaps the gentleman had the ambition to join the Union Army. There was another Camp Nelson in Kentucky where the Union trained Negro soldiers. Who knew? Maybe they'd each end up at Camp Nelson.

Tapping his foot impatiently, he waited for Alice to come back and inform him that everyone was safely stowed away under the house. As it was taking more time than he'd anticipated, he allowed his mind to wander.

Had it been a different time and a different place, he knew that he'd want to pursue a relationship with Alice. Heck, any time or place that wasn't smack dab in the middle of a war would be acceptable.

Up to this point, he'd managed to stay clear of the battlefront, but that could change at any time. It wouldn't be fair to start a courtship that he might not see through to the end.

If the war stopped this very moment, he'd latch onto Alice so fast, her head would spin. They'd take her wagon back to Pecan Hall, he'd make sure that she was inside the house safe and sound, and when daylight came, he'd go back and speak to her father about courting her.

What father would object to his daughter being courted by a soldier, a first lieutenant at that? If the war concluded in favor of the Confederate cause, there'd be balls and cotillions galore in celebration.

Assuming that Alice hadn't been introduced to society yet, he'd be more than happy to be her escort. He'd allow other young bucks to fill her dance card, provided she saved the last dance for him.

As an officer on the winning side of the war, he'd have his pick of assignments once the dust settled. He had in his possession a piece of parchment declaring him a man of the law. With years of soldiering under his belt, military law could be his specialty.

His heart was still set on moving to Texas. That state called to him. Fort Caney in Sargent, Texas, and Fort Grigsby, on the border between Louisiana and Texas, were former Union strongholds that had been abandoned by the Yankees when the war broke out.

Since that time, they'd been garrisoned to prepare for conflicts between the Confederate Army and Union Army, if the conflict ever got that far west. Marshall surmised that after the war, they'd be regarrisoned by the local Texas forces to build up defenses against Indian incursions.

He'd have a career, he'd get himself some property to homestead, then he'd get himself a wife. *Wouldn't that be something if it could be Alice?*

His infatuation with the young lady even surprised him. Back home, he'd made the acquaintance of plenty of girls. They were attracted to him like bees to honey, seemingly taken in by his pleasant visage and fine physique. That gray uniform with the officer insignia didn't hurt either.

Truth be told, those physical attributes might not have actually been what caught the girls' fancy. They talked of his fine character and how amusing he was. It wasn't like he was putting on airs, trying to make girls like him; he was just being himself. It was a heck of a lot easier than trying to be somebody else.

Though he'd had his pick of females to choose from, not one of them stood out from the crowd. Sure, there were some beauties, but they were as shallow as a mudpuddle to him. He couldn't imagine having more than a five-minute conversation with any of them.

Alice, on the other hand, was in a league of her own. Her lovely face, honey skin tone, and a body with curves in all the right places put the rest of those silly girls in a distant second place.

From what he could tell, she wasn't one to prattle on, spilling out everything that came to her mind. She thought before she spoke. Smart as a whip, learned, a practicing Catholic — *that one's for you, Mama* — a planner, and braver than she probably even realized herself.

Maybe she'd appreciate a man with a sense of humor? He couldn't picture her giggling like a schoolgirl, but he imagined that she'd enjoy some good-natured frivolity.

That's precisely what he'd like to do. Get to know her. But it didn't appear that this was the time. He spotted her approaching the conveyance, stealthily darting from tree to tree until she got to his position.

"Everyone is settled in," she said, catching her breath.

"Glad to hear that."

"You mentioned that you'd bring the wagon back to Pecan Hall. Are you sure you want to do that still? What if someone stops you along the way and asks what you're up to?"

"No one will stop a Confederate officer, trust me. Even if they did, I would just say that I'd found the abandoned wagon and was bringing it back to the plantation. It's marked on the side."

Alice nodded, and then after a moment of hesitation, words gushed out. "How can I ever thank you for your assistance?"

"It truly was my pleasure. It's not every day that I get to help a damsel in distress."

The smile she gave him was dazzling. Just as quickly, though, it disappeared. She looked down at the ground and traced a circle in the dirt with her shoe.

"Well, I guess it's time we make our *adieus*...."

"I guess," agreed Marshall. "Alice, I've enjoyed every moment we've shared today. Who knows where the winds of war will blow me, but if it's God's will, maybe this won't be the last time we see each other."

Alice tilted her head up. She didn't even attempt to hide the tears gathering on her lower eyelashes.

"That's a lovely thought, but Marshall, I'm afraid we're not meant to be together."

His head shot back in surprise. "How can you say that? We seem so compatible."

"That is true, and honestly, I've never met another man like you."

"I've never met anyone like you either."

She gave him a smile shrouded in sadness. "That's so sweet. But if you really knew everything about me, you'd want nothing to do with me."

"Impossible. From what I already know of you, I'm certain that you're just as beautiful on the inside as you are on the outside."

"That's the nicest thing anyone has ever said to me. I'll always treasure your words."

She held her hand out as if to shake his. "I need to get back to the others."

He grabbed her fine-boned hand in his. "Are you sure you can't spare a few more minutes?"

"I can't." She pulled her hand free and dabbed her eye with the bottom of her sleeve. "I must go. God bless you, First Lieutenant Marshall Kent. I hope you get everything you want in life."

With that, she picked up her skirts and fled back to the McGinnis house.

Chapter XV

Alice took a minute to compose herself before she reached for the handle to the cellar door. If Marcus saw even one trace of a tear on her cheek, he'd know that something was wrong. She'd be humiliated if he found out that she had feelings for Marshall.

What is wrong with me? She shook her head. *The first white man who treats me in a somewhat honorable fashion, and I fall head over heels for him?*

To be honest, it wasn't just that he'd been kind to her. There was so much more than that. If she had such a thing as a list of the ten qualities that she'd hope to find in a husband someday, Marshall would check off every item. He was Catholic, his *maman* raised him to respect all mankind, he was compassionate, intelligent, decisive. And he had a sense of humor, he had aspirations for his life, he was respectful, he took care of himself physically, and he was a family man.

And, my oh my, he is devilishly handsome. Not that she would have placed that on her list, as it would appear somewhat shallow, but that soldier was easy on the eyes. If he were hers, she'd never get tired of seeing that face.

That being said, he had one major flaw. He was white. Admittedly, with the tan that he sported, his skin tone wasn't that much different than hers, but there was no doubt that he was Caucasian. From his wavy chestnut-colored hair to his chiseled facial features and narrow lips, there was no disguising his

European heritage.

Even if Marshall did, by some miracle, harbor similar affectionate thoughts toward her — *and* they could ignore their racial disparity — there would be no future for them as a couple. Where could they possibly live as man and wife and not be judged by their neighbors and associates?

Of course, some states were so vast that they could do what they liked with no one being any the wiser. She was only one-quarter African, so technically, she was more Caucasian than Negro. Say they went to a state like Texas. They could be married by some municipal judge who probably wouldn't suspect a thing.

Alice pulled her shoulders back. As much as she would enjoy standing outside and dreaming of Marshall the rest of the night, she needed to see to the comfort of Marcus, Daisy and the babies.

At the present moment, there was no way of telling if Mr. McGinnis was in residence or not, so they'd have to make their stay as short as possible. She wasn't concerned about the womenfolk inside; she doubted if any of them would know how to load a pistol, let alone fire one accurately. The master of the house, on the other hand, would be likely to shoot first and ask questions later. She'd just as soon not confront the man and find out.

Little Abraham had her worried. The whiskey they'd administered to him earlier in the night was wearing off, and his coughing started up again. The croup could be deadly for someone his age. Being discovered because of his hacking could be deadly for the rest of them.

As little as he was, the coughing wasn't loud,

thankfully. But she was still concerned about proceeding to the next stop if he was ill. The evening air was damp, and traveling at night could be detrimental to his health. If only they could stay here until he'd rounded the corner. Having a sick child wasn't something that she'd factored into the escape plan. Two sick children would be even worse. Hopefully, Josiah would remain healthy.

If Mr. McGinnis was in Richmond, that would give her and the others some breathing room. Stewart and his slave catchers could tear Dallas apart block by block, but they wouldn't dare step foot on the property of a member of President Jefferson Davis' cabinet. This was just about the safest place that they could be for the time being.

Saying a quick prayer, Alice pulled open the door of the root cellar. Just as she feared, Abraham was still coughing. Daisy had the receiving blanket wrapped around him to muffle the sound, but it was still audible.

The noise that gave her more concern was Josiah's crying. Marcus shushed him as he bounced him in his arms, but that only exacerbated the child's discomfort. Instinctively, she reached out for her baby.

It seemed as though Abraham's coughing was upsetting Josiah. When even she hadn't been able to settle the infant, Alice decided to bring him outside. Maybe the fresh night air would soothe him. If the barn was empty, she could nurse him there until he fell asleep and then go back to the root cellar.

Bundling him up, Alice left the cramped underground space. The baby was still crying, so she walked as briskly as she could to the barn. He settled down as they neared the structure. She paused outside to listen for deep breathing, thinking that perhaps the stableboy was sleeping in there, but, hearing nothing, she slid the door open a crack.

Once inside, Alice made her way to the stall in the farthest corner. It was empty except for a mound of straw lining the floor. She took a seat in the corner, unbuttoned the top three buttons of her dress and proceeded to nurse Josiah.

Not a minute later, the sound of the barn door sliding open further caused her heart to skip a beat. Light filtered through to the back of the barn as a lantern was swung side to side, its beams sweeping every nook and cranny of the building.

The voice of a young woman called out softly. “Ma’am, I saw you come in here. Show yourself, I mean you no harm.”

Alice drew in her breath. Josiah, having no idea of the danger that they were in, suckled away greedily, cooing in satisfaction.

They’d been discovered. She heard the lantern scrape the floor as it was set down. The next thing she knew, a girl about her age poked her head around the stall. She was a petite thing, dressed in a frilly white nightgown that came to her ankles. Thick, dark-brown hair hung to her waist.

Her hopes that the person who’d found them was a slave hand were dashed. Between the alabaster skin and light-colored eyes, the girl was the antithesis of a person with African heritage.

Despite the intrusion, all appeared well in Josiah’s world. He was intoxicated from his mother’s warm milk and on the verge of falling asleep. Alice — mama bear instincts kicking in — was on high alert. She pulled her son closer to her chest.

The intruder peered down at them. The young lady's jaw dropped open. It was apparent what had caused the chit's consternation. With her free hand, Alice tucked a stray curl behind her ear. *How could I have forgotten to put my bonnet back on?* It was unlike her to be so careless. *That's what I get for daydreaming*, she chided herself.

Eying Josiah closer, the girl let out a gasp. Alice could only imagine what she must be thinking. *Does she assume that I'm his wet nurse? Or can she see the resemblance between the two of us and know that I'm his mother? Would she guess that we're on the run? Worse yet, she may presume that I've kidnapped the poor child.*

It wasn't long before she got her answer. The young lady stepped away from the stall and grabbed a curled-up whip hanging from a nail on the wall behind her. Brandishing the weapon in her right hand, she pointed it menacingly.

Alice's eyes widened. Shielding the baby, she looked imploringly at the girl. "Please, miss. I beseech you. Do not harm my baby."

Upon hearing those words, the girl brought her hand down and nearly let the whip slip out of her grasp. She looked closer at the two of them, bewilderment evident on her face.

Josiah started fussing again. With little else she could do, Alice unlatched him from her left side, pulled the fabric of her dress up to maintain her modesty and then tugged the right shoulder of her dress down. Repositioned, the infant greedily set to work finishing his meal.

Hasn't she ever watched someone nurse a baby before? The girl stared so rudely that Alice was beginning to feel annoyed. Finally, the chit stepped away and put the whip back in its spot.

Bending down, the young lady locked eyes with her and spoke determinedly.

"I don't know why you are in my father's barn, but I intend to find out. You must answer my questions directly and, if I suspect you are lying to me, I will summon the master of the house, and you will then be at his mercy."

Chapter XVI

The wagon was back in its place at the plantation, and from what Marshall could discern, no alarm had been raised. Once he was clear of the property, he set Maximus off in a full gallop toward town. He was bone-weary and couldn't wait to lay down on the cot in the office that doubled as his living quarters.

A day went by, and nothing seemed amiss in town. It caused Marshall to wonder if the Williams family was aware that Alice was missing yet. He'd thought for sure that the first place they'd search for her was in Dallas, seeing that it was the closest municipality.

He hadn't been asleep more than an hour the next night when he was awakened by a pounding noise. His eyes sprung open. *I knew it was too good to be true.*

Slipping on his trousers, he strode to the door. Flinging it open, he saw a man of approximately his same height, build and age, looking utterly enraged.

"What can I do for you?" asked Marshall calmy, not wishing to rile the man up any more than he already was.

"Are you First Lieutenant Kent?" the man inquired.

"I am."

"I've been told that you're in charge of this here Army unit."

"That's correct. What may I do for you?"

"I was robbed."

Since when have I become the town constable?

Keeping his annoyance in check, Marshall replied, "I'm sorry to hear that, sir. But petty theft isn't in our jurisdiction. That's what the local law enforcement is for."

"The law enforcement in this town is useless. The biggest crime they're equipped to handle is public drunkenness," the man snarled. "This is a job for the military."

"That may be so, but this matter cannot be so pressing that it needs to be dealt with immediately."

"On the contrary, it is. Time is of the essence. This property is on the run."

The hair on the back of Marshall's neck stood on end. *Must be someone from the Williams' plantation.* Looking to stall for time, he formulated some questions to keep the man talking.

"Let's start at the beginning. First off, may I get your name?"

"Stewart Williams. Owner of Pecan Hall."

Williams? The master himself.

"All right, Mr. Williams. But, before we get too far, I should inform you that it's not the job of military personnel to get involved in civic matters."

"Then what exactly are you squatting in this town for?"

It was a fair question, one that Marshall had asked himself. He racked his brain for a plausible answer.

"I'm here on behalf of Major General John George Walker, training new recruits to defend this territory if need be. Sherman and his forces are marching closer to Georgia every day."

The man was not impressed.

"I've other duties as well, but finding stolen property isn't one of them," Marshall added firmly.

"It is now," the man shot back.

Marshall stood toe to toe with his aggressor. They may be proportionally equal, but he knew that he could take the fellow in fisticuffs if it came to that. Four years of military training had honed his hand-to-hand fighting skills. Besides that, the man was in a fury. People make rash moves when they're in such a state.

Although the chap rankled him, common sense prevailed, and Marshall made the decision to act as if he'd be toeing the line. He'd rather pretend to participate in this manhunt than involve the local constable, who may actually have an interest in solving the crime.

"As you wish. Let me light the lamp, get paper and a pencil, and you can describe the missing property," said Marshall solicitously.

"There's no time for that," barked Stewart. "I'm already a day behind as I just got back into town from a business trip."

"Taking thorough notes could hasten our progress, but if you'd prefer not...."

"I'd prefer not. What do you need to know to start searching?"

"Let's start at the beginning. Where were these goods stolen from?" Marshall inquired, feigning ignorance to the fact that he wasn't talking about physical possessions but human beings.

"From my plantation."

"How did you discover the theft?"

"My overseer saw one of our wagons parked out of place. Thinking something was amiss, he checked all the slave cabins and noticed one empty."

It took everything in his power for Marshall to keep a poker face, but inside he was disappointed in himself.

He'd sworn that he'd positioned the conveyance just as he'd been instructed. How could he have bungled such a simple task? If Alice and that family were caught because of his carelessness, he'd be devastated.

"Can you describe the missing property?"

"Negroes," the man said with disgust. "We got a goliath of a man, black as night, in his mid-twenties. Then there's his lady friend, a few years younger, and she's got a baby. Kid's a few months old. They belonged to my father."

When Stewart paused, Marshall had a sliver of hope that they hadn't found out that Alice was missing too. The hope was crushed soon enough.

"They're the least of my concern. The other two pieces of property I demand be returned to me immediately as they're mine. Could be harder to track down, though. They appear to be white, but they're Negroes, just the same as the other three. It's a girl, seventeen years old, and her six-week-old son."

Marshall blinked to hide the astonishment in his eyes. He wasn't sure what astounded him more, the fact that Alice had a child or that she was a slave.

Chapter XVII

Could the girl be telling the truth? Was the master of the house truly in residence, or was she bluffing? Alice held her gaze.

"Do I make myself clear?"

"Yes, miss. I comprehend precisely," she responded icily.

Alice got the exact reaction that she'd hoped for. The girl seemed perplexed by her word choice. Nonetheless, she plowed ahead.

"You look to be a mulatto. Am I correct?"

"No, miss. My mother was a mulatto; I am a quadroon. I'm one-quarter African."

"How is it you came to be so articulate?"

Alice lifted her chin and glared at her inquisitor. "I would imagine the same way you came to be articulate, miss. I was educated."

"Educated? By whom? I'm not aware of any schools for Negro children."

"Nor am I," she replied. "I was tutored by a governess, as were my siblings."

"You do remember what I said about being truthful with me," the girl replied in a stern voice.

"Of course, I do. I am telling the truth." *Why on earth would she question my claim?*

The girl narrowed her eyes. "You had a governess, so you were raised in a family with some means. Are you a free black then?"

Alice chose not to answer. She didn't want to

incriminate herself. After a moment of silence, the girl switched to another line of questioning.

"You said the child is yours," she continued. "Do you mean the child is in your care? Are you its wet nurse? And if so, why have you taken the child from its mother?"

The nerve of this girl! "I am his mother. He rightfully belongs to me."

At that moment, Josiah detached and swung his head towards the girl's voice. Alice laid him on her knees and rebuttoned her dress. The young lady plucked up the sconce, holding it next to the baby to examine him closer. Seeing his hazel eyes, she pursed her lips together.

"This child is white," she stated emphatically. "You cannot tell me he is yours."

"I beg your pardon, miss, but I can assure you that he isn't white. He is, in fact, an octoroon."

The girl set her hands on her hips. "Have you passed yourself off as white in order to marry a white male?" she demanded to know.

It was obvious that she was putting two and two together. Seeing that Josiah was only one-eighth African, the logical conclusion would be that his father was Caucasian.

Alice set her chin and replied. "I have no husband."

The girl's mouth was agape. "Then who is the father of this child?"

"I cannot tell you."

"Why on earth not?"

Alice considered how best to answer the question. It took some time to formulate a response.

"Josiah is a sweet, innocent child, but his father is a

wicked human being. I was given to that vile man on his eighteenth birthday, just as my mother had been given to his father when that man became of age."

She paused a moment, gathering up steam. "When I discovered I was with child, I did my best to hide it from him as long as I could. He was furious when he found out — as though I were the one at fault. He demanded I get rid of it. A doctor was brought out to the plantation to take care of the problem, but by that time, the baby was too far along for him to perform his procedure. Instead, I was given a tonic to drink every night for a week. That was meant to make the baby wither away inside of me."

The young lady gawked at her, apparently dumbfounded by what she heard.

"By that time, I was far enough along that the man was disgusted by the look of my body and no longer had the desire to take me to his bed. So, I was forced to leave my position in the household as his mother's handmaid and sent to live in the shacks with the field workers. I lied to him and said I took the tonic, but I couldn't do that to my own flesh and blood — regardless of who the father was. The baby was born shortly after that, and as you can see, he is perfectly healthy. The man is expecting me to report back to the house tomorrow, but I couldn't abandon Josiah, so we left under the cover of darkness earlier tonight."

The girl appeared to be in shock. She took a step back from Alice and held her hand to her chest. "You're a fugitive?"

Chapter XVIII

Marshall's thoughts immediately returned to Alice and the statement that she'd made when they were parting ways. "If you really knew everything about me, you'd want nothing to do with me."

He'd assumed that she was referring to her African heritage, as trivial as that was in his mind. It never occurred to him that one of those babies could have belonged to her. Now that he thought about it, even though the smaller child had been bundled up as the family snuck to the McGinnis cellar, its face had been visible between the folds of the blanket.

With all that had been going on at that moment, he'd given the babe scant notice. The picture of the child flashed through his mind. His skin was lighter in color than Alice's, and he had a unique eye color. It was unusual for a Caucasian but even more unusual for a Negro. His eyes were hazel.

As he was pondering this bit of information, Stewart continued his rant.

"Are you listening?" he spat, tapping his index finger on the soldier's chest.

This caused Marshall to drop his chin down and lock eyes with Stewart. The sight caused him to freeze solid where he stood and the sound of ocean waves, so familiar from his time spent at Charleston Harbor, crashed through his brain.

Those eyes. He distinctly recognized them. Stewart's eyes were identical in color to the infant's eyes. This scoundrel was the father of Alice's child.

Anger grew inside of Marshall like he'd never

experienced before. The thought of that viper touching her infuriated him.

He slapped the man's finger from his chest.

"You set a hand on me again, and you'll rue the day you were born," Marshall grit out between clenched teeth.

"Woah," said Stewart, holding his hands up in protest. "No need to get so riled up."

Marshall stared the man down. After a few seconds of uncomfortable silence, Stewart spoke up again.

"I want you to track down those darkies," he snarled.

"Unless the man is a deserter from the Confederate Army, this is none of the Army's concern."

"You'll want to make it your concern, First Lieutenant. Before my father passed, he was one of the most distinguished landowners in Paulding County."

"What, pray tell, does that have to do with engaging assistance from the Confederate Army?"

"Whose money do you think is financing the troops mustered here?" Stewart asked with a tone of superiority.

"Let me guess. Your father's."

"Exactly. You're going to direct your men to do what I tell you, or the funding for this operation will be rescinded immediately. Do I make myself clear?"

"Loud and clear," Marshall replied. It took theatrical skills on his part to make it sound as if he were conceding. But he knew it would be better for Alice and her companions if he put himself in charge of scavenging the area. He'd do everything in his power to throw Stewart and his vigilantes off their trail.

"Where do you suggest we start?" he asked the man, trying to assess his tracking skills.

"The wagon was misplaced. That makes me think that the fugitives had an accomplice. A white one, I'm guessing. Someone who could drive a horse-drawn vehicle down a country road without drawing any attention to himself."

The guy was more clever than Marshall had given him credit for.

"That could make sense."

"I would say that he either dropped them off in town at a safehouse or left them on a main road headed north to set out on foot. They have more than a twenty-four-hour headstart on us, but we can easily make up the time on horseback."

As much as Marshall didn't want to aid the investigation, he needed to know something for his own peace of mind.

"You have your dogs after them?"

"They're in the hands of the overseers now. Only problem is, we haven't got a lot of scent to go on. They escaped with everything they owned."

That wasn't much, as Marshall well knew. Didn't seem that the owners of Pecan Hall were overly generous with their help. As far as he could tell, a knapsack held the possessions of all five of the fugitives, with room to spare.

"Didn't help that they were transported by wagon. Their scent dispersed at the border of our property. We're hoping the slave hounds will pick it up somewhere in town,"

The man's hazel eyes darkened. "I'll tell you what, when I find the person here who's aiding and abetting runaways, I'll form a lynch mob and string him up myself."

Something gives me a feeling that Stewart's had some experience in that area before.

At that moment, Marshall thanked God that he'd had the good sense to get the group out of town when he did. Their chances of being undetected in a town this size were slim. They couldn't have holed up at the Quaker homestead forever.

"Where do my men fit into this equation?" asked Marshall.

"I suggest they go door to door and talk to every resident to see if they can get any information out of them."

"Out of the question. My soldiers have better things to do than waste their time calling on each and every citizen in this municipality."

The man narrowed his eyes at him, but Marshall gave no sign of backing down.

"Well then, at least find me the soldier who had the overnight patrol the night before last. As quiet as it is here, if a wagon rolled into town in the dead of night, he certainly would have heard something."

"There is no overnight patrol," noted Marshall.

"Fine. Then get me the man who had the last shift. I'll question him myself."

Marshall glared into the other man's eyes. "You're looking at him."

Chapter XIX

It got to the point that Alice was starting to feel sorry for the young lady who'd discovered her. Finding escaped slaves on her family's property didn't seem to sit too well with her.

"Miss...," the girl began haltingly, "what name do you go by?"

"I'd prefer not to reveal that if you don't mind, not until I discover your true character."

The astounded look on the girl's face almost caused Alice to burst out in laughter. She could just imagine what she was thinking. It didn't take long to know for sure.

"Listen, missy. I will have you know that my character is above reproach. Our family is well-respected in this town and, personally, I intend to say vows to the Church later this year. So, I'd appreciate it if you didn't question my morals."

"Yes, miss," she answered in a less-than-conciliatory tone.

"Now that we have that settled, let me reassure you, even though as a dutiful citizen I should turn you over to the proper authorities, I have decided to let you go. You may take a few minutes to attend to your child, but then I would ask that you vacate this building."

A feeling of relief washed over Alice. "Thank you, miss. I truly am grateful for your leniency."

"You may call me Miss Brigid, if you'd care to. And your name is?"

Considering the girl's kind offer, she chose to answer

truthfully. "Alice."

"Well, it was a pleasure getting to know you, Alice, but I assume you'd like to put some distance between yourself and this town before the sun rises, so we should say our *adieus*."

Alice couldn't hide her consternation.

"*Adieu*. That means goodbye in French."

"*Je comprends*," she replied haughtily. *Does this woman think I'm some country bumpkin?*

The answer seemed less-than-satisfactory to her. "Is there something else wrong? Am I not being generous enough with your fate?"

"You truly are, Miss Brigid, but it's a bit more complicated than that."

"How's that?"

She peered straight into the young lady's eyes. "It isn't just me."

"Obviously, I know you have the baby to think of."

"It's not just Josiah either. It's the others."

"What others?" questioned Brigid with a note of alarm in her voice.

"It's my brother and his intended and their son," Alice replied, keeping her voice low.

"What about them?"

"They're here too," she said.

Brigid put her hand to her chest, backed against the rough barn wall and glanced around wildly. "In here?"

"No, miss. In the root cellar."

"Root cellar? Our root cellar?" she asked in disbelief.

Alice nodded.

"What are they doing there?"

"It's a depot," she answered in a hushed tone.

Comprehension washed over Brigid's countenance.

"Please, Miss Brigid, have compassion on my family," Alice begged. "If you knew the despicable conditions all the colored folks endure on the plantation, you would have pity on us. Shall I show you the scars on my back from being whipped by my master for his own sadistic satisfaction?"

That was an outright lie, but it had its intended effect. The blood drained from Brigid's face.

"You say you're a female of principles and that you intend to devote your life to the Church," continued Alice. "Are you not familiar with First Corinthians, chapter seven, verses twenty-two and twenty-three? 'You see, anyone who was called in the Lord while a slave, is a free man of the Lord; and in the same way, anyone who was free when called is a slave of Christ. You have been bought at a price; do not be slaves now to any human being.'"

With no response forthcoming, she continued, "We don't want to get you embroiled in this situation, Miss Brigid, but I'm pleading for your help. My nephew is only a few months old, and something isn't right with him. His breathing is impaired, and we don't know if he can tolerate the damp night air. We're just requesting a couple of days for him to recuperate before we resume our journey."

After a moment's hesitation as she perhaps weighed her options, Brigid responded, "You may stay, but as soon as the baby's health is stabilized, you must leave at once."

Relief washed over Alice. She tilted her head up toward the barn roof, thanking God and her guardian angel for watching over her.

With the baby balanced in one arm, she got up and

followed Brigid as she proceeded towards the barn door. Stopping before they exited, the young lady turned toward her. "I will do what I can to make you comfortable for the remainder of your stay. The members of your party are hungry and thirsty, I would imagine. I'll fetch some libations and put together a poultice to rub on the baby's chest to help clear his lungs. Now get yourself back into the root cellar. I'll be down there shortly."

Some fifteen minutes later, Brigid appeared at the cellar door with a parcel in one hand and a copper pitcher in the other. Alice acknowledged her from her spot on the floor next to Daisy, who was holding Abraham protectively.

Marcus showed concern when Brigid reached for his child. Alice gave Daisy a look of encouragement. Reluctantly she handed the baby to the white girl.

Brigid set the pitcher and the cloth parcel on a shelf. She pulled a poultice from the fabric and, lifting the baby's gown, slowly rubbed the concoction on his chest. Her fingers were trembling as she went about her ministrations.

The sensation must have been soothing to the child as he gave her a big toothless grin. Brigid smiled back at him. Satisfied with her work, she lowered the gown and handed him to Daisy, who nodded her head in thanks.

Alice stood up to introduce the occupants of the space to Brigid but was shushed by the young woman. Apparently, she had no desire to get any more entangled in their situation than she already was.

Chapter XX

Stewart narrowed his eyes at Marshall.

"Looks like we've found the ideal place to start."

"What are you implying?"

"Not implying anything," said Stewart. "Just have a few questions to ask."

"Be my guest."

"You see any people moseying around town the night before last in a wagon pulled by a single horse?"

"Obviously, I saw plenty of people out and about. If by the word *people*, you're implying enslaved people, I would say not. It seems to me that a person in that particular situation would take the necessary precautions to avoid detection. Especially from the military."

"True enough. So, maybe you didn't see an entire family gallivanting through the streets. However, it'd be easy enough to hide folks in the back of a vehicle and have just one person visible. The fugitives stole all the bedding from their cabin, most likely as a means to conceal themselves."

Stole? Did Stewart's slaves not have any personal possessions? That'd be one more accusation leveled against Alice and the others if they got caught and went to trial. If there even was such a thing as a trial for apprehended runaways. More than likely, the plantation owner would play the role of judge, attorney and jury. They'd never stand a chance.

While it would sound foolhardy for a slaveholder to exterminate some of his most valuable possessions, sometimes such things were done to discourage other slaves from attempting such an unwise endeavor themselves. Of course, there was always the option of whipping the slave. That might just make them wish that they were dead. The thought sickened Marshall.

"The teenage girl," continued Stewart, "she most likely would have been the one driving the wagon. She's a clever one. If I had to guess, she was the mastermind behind the plan."

"A girl? That's hard to imagine. If she's like any of the young ladies that I know, the last thing she'd want to do is put her life in mortal danger. Especially helping other people. As a whole, they seemed more interested in themselves than the rest of humanity."

"She probably has the misguided notion of saving her family."

"Oh, they're all kin, then?"

"That fellow Marcus watches over her like she's his kid sister. But one glance at the pair, and you'd know they're not related. They couldn't look any different from each other if they tried."

"You're telling me she'd put her life on the line for some man who isn't even related to her? That just doesn't sound right to me."

"You don't know this girl," said Stewart emphatically.

Or so you think.

"If you were acquainted with her, you'd realize she's unlike any female — white or Negro — that you'd ever encountered before. She has a soft spot in her heart for all living creatures. If she found a bird in the woods with a broken wing, she'd take care of that thing until it was well enough to be on its own. And she knew how, too. She grew up alongside me and my sister. We had the same governess tutoring us. Of course, she took to learning more than Susanna and I did. Never saw her around the plantation without a book in her hand."

The man glanced off in the distance as if savoring a cherished memory. This change in his demeanor puzzled Marshall. He waited for Stewart to continue.

"That girl could probably best anyone her age in a test of knowledge — regardless of their gender. When you're around her, she's quiet, always observing and tucking away every tidbit of information that comes her way. On top of that, she carries herself like royalty. Some say she's of noble African blood. I've never heard of such a thing. But she has a refined beauty that's unequaled. So, perhaps there is some truth to that."

This turn in their interchange was starting to make Marshall feel uncomfortable. He couldn't believe his ears. If he hadn't known the person about whom Stewart spoke, he would have sworn that he was describing some young lady that he was wooing. Was it possible that he had feelings for Alice? Could the man actually have a heart, after all? It was difficult to imagine.

Marshall squeezed his eyes shut to brush away the images forming in his mind. There was no doubt that Stewart was the father of Alice's baby. He was her master, and he'd violated her. But, did he, in some perverse sense, imagine that he was showing her affection by his actions? The thought was nothing short of appalling.

Another thought came to him that was even more alarming. Maybe Alice had willingly been in a relationship with him. Perhaps things went sour when she got pregnant. Those things did happen.

Both men were momentarily lost in their own thoughts. After a moment, Marshall spoke up.

"Williams, regardless of the girl's unusual attractiveness, I can't see how she'd think she'd get away with driving a vehicle into town without being stopped and questioned by some authority. A Negro woman commanding a wagon by herself would be highly unusual."

"That's the kicker," Stewart replied. "A person would hardly know that she was of slave stock. She doesn't handle herself with an air of submissiveness. She's only a quarter Negro. Her skin isn't much darker than yours or mine."

"You don't say," replied Marshall, a manufactured note of surprise in his voice.

"Now that you've got the details, did you run across a person such as her in Dallas yesterday?"

Marshall knew darn well that lying, like all sins, was an offense against God and a rejection of His perfect justice and love. The most serious sins were mortal sins that destroyed the grace of God in the heart of the sinner, cut off their relationship with Him, and turned them away from their creator.

Thankfully, lying fell into the category of venial sins. While technically they didn't cut one off from Christ, they weakened grace in the soul and damaged a person's relationship with God. *Wouldn't Mama be impressed to know that I was actually paying attention in catechism class?*

Mortal. Venial. It made no difference at this point in the game. He'd make amends at Confession the next time he got there, which hopefully would be before he left Dallas.

The perfect response came to him in a flash. "I can't say that I did," he replied, which was God's honest truth.

"You sure about that, Kent?"

"You know this town, Williams. Nothing to see here. With all the men off to war, all you've got are ladies, kids and old folks."

Stewart gave him a look that indicated that he didn't entirely accept his answer, but, nonetheless, he gave up questioning Marshall.

"Can you put extra men out on patrol?"

"I can spare a couple. No use in riling up the whole town. I'll have them canvas the area after first light."

"Good enough."

Thankfully that was the end of the conversation. Marshall had his hand on the doorknob and was just about to swing the door shut when Stewart held his hand up to halt him.

"One last thing, Kent. Seeing as you're first in command around here, I want you accompanying me in the search. I'll be back in a couple hours."

Mama was right. Lying will get you nowhere.

Chapter XXI

After Brigid departed the root cellar, Alice spread out a quilt on the floor so that she could lay down for a couple hours until Josiah needed to be fed again. With the baby tucked next to her, she did her best to unwind from what had been an exhausting day.

Try as she might, she couldn't get her eyes to stay shut. Thoughts from the last week flitted through her brain and demanded that she pay them attention. Rather than trying to force herself to sleep, she took the advice that her *maman* had told her many times as a child. She would count her blessings instead of sheep.

Blessings had flowed abundantly from God the last few days as she'd prepared for their escape. She'd felt His hand upon her as she assembled the pieces to make their flight possible.

In some ways, it seemed as though she and Marcus and the others were reliving a story straight from the Bible. On Passover, Jewish families recount the Hebrews' flight from slavery. They had a miraculous escape when Moses parted the Red Sea. *Who's to say we can't have a miraculous escape as well?*

While everything the past few days had gone relatively according to plan, the one thing that she would never have factored into her formulations was meeting Marshall. She could see him clearly in her thoughts. That wavy brown hair which brushed the top of his collar, the clean-shaven chiseled face with a cleft in his chin that made him wickedly attractive, the hazel eyes so close in shade to her Josiah's, his tall, lean frame with muscles barely concealed by his gray uniform.

For some reason, he was meant to appear in her life; she was sure of it. But, was this just a chance encounter so that he could be of assistance to her? Like a guardian angel making an earthly stop to take care of its ward?

Is this all there will be for Marshall and me? No matter how much she desired for more to come of this, Alice couldn't figure out how that would be possible. Maybe someday, decades from now, men and women of different races could have lives together, but she just didn't see that happening anytime soon.

Of course, with a war going on, few people of any race were saying vows. Men of marrying age were killing each other off by the thousands. How many would be left in the end was impossible to tell.

That thought was dismaying, so she opted to think back to a story that her mother had told her so many times that she'd memorized it word for word. When Josiah was old enough to understand, she would pass it along to him. It was the story of their ancestors in Africa and how they were forced to live in the New World.

Their family came from Burundi, a landlocked nation in the heart of Africa that was founded by a man named Cambarantama some 300 years ago. Ntare IV Rutaganzwa Rugamba, Alice's great-grandfather, who was the son of King Mwambutsa I Mbariza, ruled the country from 1796 until 1850. Under his reign, the kingdom doubled in size.

The king, known as the *mwami*, headed a princely aristocracy that owned most of the land and required a tribute from local herders and farmers.

For centuries along the West African coast, countless Africans were sold into slavery and shipped across the Atlantic Ocean to the Americas. The middlemen were European slave traders based in forts in Ghana and other western African nations.

The Europeans, almost without exception, did not capture the slaves themselves. Africans, usually kings, chiefs or wealthy merchants, enslaved fellow Africans, sending them to the coast to be sold to white merchants.

Centuries before Europeans arrived in Africa, it was common for slaves to be sold and taken by caravans across the Sahara Desert. Slavery was an accepted practice on the continent, but slaves had rights and protection under the law and were able to move about as they pleased. They became part of families' households.

Once warring began between neighboring African countries, prisoners were sold to slave traders in exchange for European guns. The kings and chiefs had no idea how brutal life was for the slaves shipped overseas. If they had, the barbaric practice might have ended earlier.

Her grandmother Asma, the youngest daughter of the king, had been captured by soldiers from The Kingdom of Kongo. She had been herded onto a ship called Port au Prince that France had built in the late 1700s that had been refitted for the slave trade by The British Royal Navy after its capture.

The ship dropped off its cargo, including the teenage

princess, in Haiti. One year later, in 1806, the vessel was anchored at a Tongan island. Local inhabitants massacred half her crew and scuttled her.

If that massacre had happened before my grandmother was kidnapped, mayhap I would be living life now as royalty instead of as a slave.

Chapter XXII

Even after spending several hours with the man, Marshall still couldn't figure Stewart out. Once the man had gotten over his tirade, he seemed personable enough. The fellows who accompanied him enjoyed his company from what he could tell. He had a supply of jokes to keep his sidekicks chuckling all day.

The slave trackers' mood as they searched home by home was odd, to say the least. As nonchalant as they were, a person would think that they were on a scavenger hunt. *Is chasing down human beings just another pastime for them?*

The group of men was methodical in their tracking. Marshall had been under the assumption that they were friends and neighbors of the Williams family, but after observing them at work, he'd put money on it that they were professional bounty hunters.

Marshall trekked side by side with Stewart for a good part of the day. As tedious as it was, he was glad to be doing it so he could have the man in his sights and see where the search led. The words attributed to the infamous Chinese general and military strategist Sun Tzu came to mind. "Keep your friends close and your enemies closer." Solid advice under his current circumstances.

After five hours with the man — who was cockier than all get out — the jokes wore thin, and he was mighty tired of listening to the blowhard who started each sentence with the word "I." He may have ranked at the top of his mama's list, but he was considerably lower on Marshall's.

The one silver lining to the cloud that hung over his head all day was that Marshall learned more about Stewart's background, and with that, Alice's as well. The man just loved to listen to himself talk. He chattered away as they traveled the main road leading north from town.

Apparently, Alice was the third generation of women from her family to be enslaved by the Williams family. Her grandmother had come to be in possession of Stewart's grandfather, Albert Williams, when he owned a plantation in Haiti. He'd amassed considerable wealth there, growing sugar and coffee off the backs of slave labor.

Stewart told Marshall about Asma, even though he'd been young when she passed away. She had been his grandmother's handmaid — or lady in waiting as "*grandmere*" liked to call her — since the two women had been teenagers.

Miss Asma had come directly from Africa. Her father ruled the country of Burundi for more than fifty years and had passed away perhaps a dozen years ago. Asma was born of his most favored wife and thus quite beloved to him.

The man was a powerful ruler, and his kingdom increased substantially under his reign. That caused jealously amongst neighboring countries. Their neighbors in Kongo had discovered a lucrative living could be made assisting white men in the slave trade. The European slave traffickers didn't know the continent nor have the means of protection to go into the inner countries on the continent, so they hired African men to do the dirty work for them.

Thus, Asma, and numerous members of her household, were kidnapped and transported to the Ivory Coast on the western shore of Africa. From there, they were shipped to Port-au-Prince, Haiti, via — coincidentally enough — the British Royal Navy ship HMS Port au Prince.

Asma was fifteen years old when she arrived in Port-au-Prince. Albert Williams happened to be in the market for more slaves that fateful day when she was paraded in front of potential buyers and put up for auction. That man was quite taken with her exquisite features and knew royalty when he saw it. He paid the unheard-of sum of one-hundred dollars for the girl.

That young lady was a smart one. She spoke her native language Kirundi and, within months of arriving in Haiti, was fluent in both French and English as well. By the time Albert Williams married Stewart's grandmother, Francis Byron — who put on airs because she was second-cousin twice removed of the famous British poet and politician Lord George Byron — he had fathered one bastard child with Asma and had another on the way.

That was to be the last child born of Albert and Asma. In 1798 the man lost his life in the Haitian slave revolt. At that time, Stewart's father Etienne — the only child sired by Albert with his wife Francis — was six years old. As young as he was, he remembered every detail of that fateful day. He'd been an eyewitness to his father's stabbing by a Negro wielding a knife fashioned from a sugarcane stalk.

The uprising was crushed soon enough, and when the final flames died out, the murderers were rounded up. Etienne stood alongside his mother and watched the beheading of the man who'd taken his father's life.

At that point, Stewart had paused in his narrative to reflect on the incident. "I've made it my life's mission to avenge my grandfather's assassination," he stated, all joviality wiped from his face. "In my mind, one African is the same as any other African. They all carry the guilt of the slayer who stole the patriarch from our family."

Carrying that much anger toward an entire race of people could not be healthy, Marshall thought. It sickens a person's mind. That incident had happened nearly seventy years ago. It was time that the Williams family put it behind them. Of course, seeing that slavery was still an institution in the South, how could they? They were surrounded by people that evoked that haunting memory every day.

Stewart continued his story. "My *grand-mere* could not stand the thought of living in Haiti after her husbands' death. She made orders to replenish their stock of slaves and then sailed to America. With the profit from selling the plantation in Haiti, she was able to buy a similar-sized property in Georgia."

The area had appealed to her because there was a thriving Catholic community there, he noted. "At that time, the owner of Pecan Hall had just passed away. As he'd been a lifelong bachelor and had no children, the property came on the market. With The Church of the Purification of the Blessed Virgin Mary located only three miles away in Dallas, it seemed the ideal location to resettle her family."

Marshall was beginning to wonder how long the man could talk without taking a breath. Alas, he finally did but immediately picked up the story where he'd left off.

"My father met my mother at that church. Mother was from the Maryland English. As a matter of fact, they were one of the founding families of the Church of the Purification of the Blessed Virgin Mary. That second child born to Asma was Alice's mother, Célia, or Cecilia as we called her. Trained as a handmaid, she had been a gift to my mother from my father when *ma mere* became mistress of the plantation."

The next revelation was chilling. "Following my grandfather's precedent, my father was presented with a gift to celebrate his coming of age as well. The 'association' between him and Célia produced Alice."

Marshall's eyes widened. Putting the pieces of the puzzle together, he realized that the woman Stewart's father impregnated — Alice's mother — had actually been the man's half-sister. The thought was repugnant, to say the least. As was the thought that immediately followed. Alice was Stewart's half-sister as well. *The apple doesn't fall far from the tree.*

Stewart grinned. "Alice, *ma petite princesse*, became my possession on my eighteenth birthday. Best gift I ever got."

Princess? Marshall vacillated between the desire to cover his ears to block out any further words from the man or to haul back and slug him. Stewart told the tale as if he were detailing the leaves on his family tree, not speaking of a cycle of abuse towards women perpetuated by the men in his family.

Chapter XXIII

Alice's ears perked up. The sun had barely risen, and yet she could hear a conveyance pulling into the yard. She peeked through the small window in the cellar to see what was going on.

Footsteps pounded overhead, and a door in the back of the house creaked open and then slammed against the doorframe.

"Father, it's so wonderful that you're back," she heard Brigid say, enunciating each word in an elevated tone.

Father? Trepidation washed over Alice. Mr. McGinnis was in the employ of the Confederate president. If he found them on his property, they'd be strung up for sure.

"I'm certainly glad to see you too, my daughter, but is there some reason you're speaking so loudly? You might not only awaken the household but the dead as well."

"My apologies, sir. I'm just excited to see you," Brigid said in a more subdued tone.

"I can imagine you're anxious to hear what news I bring you about your vocation. But it certainly can wait until morning."

There was a pause in the conversation. As she could only see Brigid's feet, Alice tried to imagine the girl's reaction.

"But, since you're here, I'll fill you in," the man conceded. "I had a considerable amount of work to do for President Davis, but I made time to research appropriate religious orders for you. I've come up with the ideal situation."

After a moment, he continued. "As you may recall, I was looking for an order that is well-established, has an impeccable reputation, and yet is a reasonable distance from here. But I also sought out an organization that performed acts of charity, like St. Brigid of Kildare, in whose honor you were named."

She could just imagine the man pulling a sheet of paper from his overcoat. He cleared his throat and began to read. "In my research, I learned about Catherine McAuley, an Irish Catholic laywoman, who in the early part of this century, recognized the many needs of poor people in Ireland. She was determined that she and other women like her could make a difference in the lives of those unfortunates. So, she spent her inheritance to open a house of mercy in Dublin in 1827 to shelter and educate women and girls. While she originally intended to assemble a lay corps of Catholic social workers, she was instructed by the Archbishop of Dublin to establish a religious congregation."

Clearing his throat, he continued on. "In 1831, she and two companions became the first Sisters of Mercy. Nuns from their order arrived in the United States in 1843."

Nuns? The man is encouraging his daughter to take up a religious vocation, and he doesn't even know the difference between a sister and a nun? Alice rolled her eyes.

"Their enthusiasm for ministering to the sick and poor brought so many new members that ten years ago, they established communities in New York City, Chicago, San Francisco and Little Rock. With the war continuing on, the good sisters felt it necessary to expand their operations into Georgia, so they opened a community in Cartersville. As you know, that's less than a day's ride from here."

Alice waited with bated breath to see where the monologue would lead.

"Just so you're aware, the process of becoming a sister takes several years," said Mr. McGinnis. "During that time, you and the community will mutually discern whether God is calling you to be a sister. You will pray, you will learn, you will study theology and minister alongside the other women."

"Yes, Father."

"I want you to go back to bed now," he replied in a stern voice. "Tomorrow, you will pack your things. The following morning Jeremiah will drive you to Cartersville. Fate is on our side; you'll be able to enroll immediately. The summer term begins next week."

There was no sound from Brigid.

"Off you go, young lady. I need to get some sleep myself, so let's not dillydally out here anymore and chance waking the girls. They'd be bright-eyed and bushy-tailed, ready to start their antics for the day. I could use some peace and quiet for a few hours."

She must have given the man some acknowledgment as the next thing that Alice heard was the back door opening once again, albeit less energetically than earlier.

If Brigid is leaving the day after tomorrow, then we must leave as well. Alice prayed that baby Abraham's coughing would diminish before they departed, or he could give them all away.

Chapter XXIV

Being bossed around by Stewart brought Marshall back to his days as a fourth classman at The Citadel. The military academy was self-governed, so the upperclassmen assumed leadership roles and ruled over the knobs.

As every cadet was expected to join the armed forces after graduation, military training was mandatory at each grade level. A typical day included reveille at five-thirty for fourth classmen, six o'clock formation for third classmen, and seven o'clock formation for upperclassmen, followed by breakfast in the mess hall, and classes from eight until noon, after which students dropped into formation to march back to mess hall for lunch.

The second half of the day was spent in the classroom from one until five o'clock. After supper, the next four hours were spent in study hall. Curfew, with campus gates locked, was at eleven o'clock sharp.

Every Friday, all the cadets participated in the parade on campus. As many miles as he'd marched in those years, he'd never grown tired of hearing "I Wish I Were in Dixie Land," or "Dixie" as it was more commonly known. The song stirred a sense of patriotism in him. To this day, the beginning notes of the song still gave him chills.

Like his fellow fourth classmen, Marshall entered The Citadel with the rank of cadet private. Second-year students, the third classmen, filled all cadet corporal ranks, serving as assistant squad leaders and clerks. Third-year students, second classmen, were promoted to cadet sergeant ranks, from squad leaders to the Regimental Sergeant Major.

Fourth-year students earned the highest positions. The Regimental Commander held the rank of Cadet Colonel; Battalion Commanders and Regimental Executive Officers were Cadet Lieutenant Colonels; Regimental Staff Officers and Battalion Executive Officers were Cadet Majors; and Company Commanders and Battalion Staff Officers were Cadet Captains. Company Executive Officers and select company staff positions were Cadet First Lieutenants, and Platoon Leaders and remaining company staff positions were Cadet Second Lieutenants.

Life at a military school wasn't easy by any means, especially for the knobs. But, as the saying went, misery loves company, so at least Marshall was able to share his torment with the other fourth classmen in his barracks.

Tradition was everything at The Citadel. The code of conduct was strict and every cadet was expected to follow the honor code. One lesson that Marshall learned the hard way was to never glance up when taking an exam. As innocent as the movement had been, it was cause to be accused of cheating.

Cheating, lying, cutting classes and sneaking back onto the campus after hours were serious infractions. If a young man was caught in a lie, they were severely punished. They had to undertake a "tour," and not a leisurely one at that. This consisted of walking back and forth a set distance while holding a rifle overhead. A cadet could be assigned as many as 100 tours for each honor code violation.

One thing that the cadets actually did anticipate with

eagerness — in the midst of the never-ending marching and studying — was attending dances that The Citadel sponsored. The guests of honor were young ladies from the Charleston area. While the merrymaking didn't happen nearly as often as Marshall would have liked, it certainly helped him get through some of the tougher days that he'd had to endure.

First classmen had a major influence on how the school was run. With the authority vested in them by the school board, they essentially ran the academy. It was a joyous day when Marshall finally reached that milestone himself and was promoted to Second Lieutenant.

While other classmates dreamed of moving up the ranks from lieutenant to captain, major, lieutenant colonel, colonel and general in the Confederate Army, he had no aspirations to have a military career. He was satisfied to have reached the rank of First Lieutenant upon graduation.

Regardless of the rank, or lack thereof, Marshall would forever be grateful for the stellar education he'd received while attending The Citadel. Between that and the leadership skills he'd acquired, he was well-prepared for life after school—particularly when unexpected events occurred, such as what he'd experienced over this past week.

Chapter XXV

Alice had spoken with Brigid each time the young lady ducked into the cellar to drop off provisions. During the course of their conversations, Alice was apprised of Brigid's background, life at the McGinnis house, and information about the folks working for their family.

The night before Brigid was to depart for Cartersville, Alice, Marcus, Daisy and the babies were moved to the barn. Just before daybreak the next morning, the McGinnis handyman Jeremiah slipped into the barn. He was said to be the most trusted person in their employ.

"Employ" was an odd term, considering that Alice was fairly certain that the man was enslaved just as she had been. As well-treated as he appeared to be, he still carried himself with the demeanor of a man who was working on someone else's terms, not his own.

Giving her a cursory glance, Jeremiah placed an oversized trunk onto the floor of the barn. He stepped outside twice, each time coming back with a matching trunk. Unceremoniously, he dumped out the contents of all the chests, seeming not to care that items of women's clothing were strewn about the straw-covered floor.

With the covers open, Alice noted that several holes had been drilled into the bottom of each trunk. Eyes widened, she realized what Brigid's escape plan for them was. The thought of being crammed inside that dark and stuffy container for four hours caused her no small amount of concern.

There was scant time to give it any thought as Jeremiah motioned for them to position themselves inside the trunks. Marcus — because of his size — had one to himself, and the young women each shared a trunk with their babies.

Alice willed herself not to be claustrophobic and laid down on the bottom of her assigned trunk in a fetal position; Josiah snuggled next to her. The two little ones had been doused with the whiskey that Brigid provided. They were inebriated enough to sleep for several hours. The thought of drugging her own child was reprehensible, but it had to be done.

Dresses and various undergarments were tossed over her and Josiah. Jeremiah shut the cover of the trunk and then buckled the leather straps to keep it secure. It was pitch black inside. Alice took several deep breaths to calm herself.

Within minutes, she was jostled as the trunk was lifted, she assumed by Jeremiah and another strong man. They shuffled out of the barn and, on the count of three, the trunk was deposited onto the back of the coach. Two more thuds assured her that Marcus and Daisy were on board as well.

Moments later, Alice heard Brigid and her family come outside and approach the vehicle.

"Why in God's name are you bringing three trunks with you to the convent, young lady?" Mr. McGinnis demanded. "You know you're taking a vow of poverty, do you not?"

Alice's breath caught in her throat.

"Of course, Father," Brigid replied reassuringly. "Those trunks are filled with all my worldly goods. I intend to offer them to the sisters when I get there – they can donate them to the poor."

"And what exactly will the underprivileged do with ball gowns, may I ask?"

"The same thing I did," said Brigid in a light tone. "Wear them. Besides, they aren't all gowns. There are day frocks and other practical things like shoes and capes and undergarments."

"Women," he muttered. "Brigid, if, God forbid, you do not profess your final vows, I am not replacing the items you've donated. You may want to think twice before you give everything away."

"I am comfortable with my decision, sir," she said resolutely.

"Good, because there is no changing your mind at this point," he responded.

Brigid must have nodded in acknowledgment because the next thing that Alice heard was her bidding farewell to her younger sisters and her mother.

"I pray you've found the ideal situation, dear, and that the life of a religious suits you," her *maman* said lovingly. "If things don't work out, know you'll always be welcome here."

A snort came from her father. "Mrs. McGinnis, don't plant ideas in her head. We've thought this whole thing through from every angle. Of course, it will work out as it should," her father asserted, in what was decidedly a contradiction from his earlier statement.

"I expect you to attend to your studies and follow the example set by the good women who have been charged with your training. The Lord will show you that you've made the proper choice."

"Yes, Father."

"Godspeed on your journey, daughter."

"Thank you, sir."

"Off you go," he directed.

"Jeremiah, get her there safely. I'll expect to see you back here by mid-afternoon."

"Yes, master," said the man.

Now, if that isn't evidence that Jeremiah was owned by Mr. McGinnis, then nothing is. How could his own daughter not realize that her family was involved in slavery?

The bench creaked as Brigid and Jeremiah took their seats. A crack of the whip set the horses in motion.

Hours later, nearing their destination, Alice listened intently as Brigid spelled out her strategy to Jeremiah. She had a plan for the escaped slaves when they arrived at the Sisters of Mercy motherhouse.

Chapter XXVI

Spending the entire day searching Dallas top to bottom had proven to be fruitless. *Thank heavens.* The hounds could pick up no scent on any road leading north. While slaves had been known to escape to Florida to make their homes in the swamps, given Dallas' geographical location in the northern part of Georgia, Stewart told Marshall that he surmised that the fugitives would be making their way toward Kentucky.

That state had officially declared its neutrality at the beginning of the war. Subsequently, a failed attempt by General Leonida Polk to claim the state for the Confederacy caused the Kentucky legislature to petition the Union Army for assistance. Since 1862, the state had been largely under Union control.

As the border between slave states and non-slave states, and with its unique geography — the only state surrounded by rivers on three sides — Kentucky created the ideal sanctuary for slaves escaping Confederate territory.

The mighty Mississippi formed its western border, the Ohio River was its northern border, and the big Sandy River and Tug Fork ran along the eastern edge of the state. The Ohio River was considered to be the River Jordan. If fugitives got that far, they were virtually free.

Slaveholding had not been abolished in Kentucky. However, there were scores of free blacks living there who were more than happy to help a fellow African escape their chains of bondage.

Knowing that Alice and her kin were holed up at the McGinnis house, which was just beyond the western edge of town, Marshall encouraged Stewart and his men to continue combing routes leading north.

He wondered how long the man would search before he gave up. The Williams family owned plenty of slaves. He'd seen the cabins scattered across the property of Pecan Hall. How much did Alice mean to him? What kind of time and energy would he be willing to expend searching for her? If he found the other escapees, would he be satisfied and return home with them and let her be?

God forbid, but if he actually did track Alice down, what would be her fate? He didn't see Stewart withholding punishment, no matter what his feelings were toward her. Would he be lenient with the whip to avoid desecrating her body? He shuddered at the thought of the leather straps biting into her smooth skin.

Regardless, Marshall wouldn't know either way. When he and Alice had parted ways, they were both realistic enough to know that it was a permanent break. As he was scheduled to relocate to Little Rock in the morning, the whole situation would be long behind him twenty-four hours from now.

When he was finally able to disengage from Stewart and his nonstop one-sided conversation, he made his way back to his office to prepare the abode for the next officer who'd be taking his place.

As he tidied the area up — doing his best to organize the stack of paperwork that, thankfully, he wouldn't have to deal with anymore — he thought more about the slave trade. The practice was so ingrained into the society in which he'd grown up, that he hadn't actually given it much thought before.

His friends in Charleston had fathers who were in the trades — blacksmithing, construction, manufacturing or importing like his father. None of them lived on plantations. The closest he'd ever gotten to one was when he'd gone up the drive of Pecan Hall.

While Negro men and women were a common sight around his hometown, the folks he saw were working-class people, going about their business as any white person would. At a glance, you wouldn't know if they were free blacks or enslaved, occupied on behalf of their masters. Marshall hadn't given them much notice. They were just part of the citizenry.

Life was different on plantations, he'd heard. Working the fields from dawn to dusk, six days a week, if not seven, was backbreaking. He really didn't know what went on behind the scenes. Did the slaves live as family units, have time off for holidays, or get to observe Sunday as a day of rest as the good Lord had admonished?

It made him wish that he'd had more time with Alice. Apart from the obvious reason of enjoying the company of a lovely woman, it would be intriguing to hear her speak of life on her plantation. Even though she'd been raised in the manor house with the Williams' legitimate children, she must have been privy to everything that went on at Pecan Hill, inside and out.

Like any help, he imagined the folks talked amongst themselves, relaying tidbits of gossip — be it about the owners and their families or the folks laboring outdoors.

If he had to guess, Alice wouldn't be the sort of person to spread gossip. As Stewart had mentioned, she was one to watch and absorb, keeping her thoughts private. That, in and of itself, certainly placed her head and shoulders above the young ladies with whom he'd interacted in his life.

Not that the males were any better. In secondary school, he and his companions had idle time enough to waste talking about their circle of friends, neighbors and the local townsfolk. Throw in a few political conversations here and there, the ever-fascinating discussion about girls — particularly those daring enough to flash an ankle to the pack of male wolves surrounding them — and you've got the makings of a solid discussion.

Interest in such things didn't die down once he got to The Citadel, but the cadets' days were so structured that they had almost no free time. At lights out, most of them were too exhausted to even say their nightly prayers, let alone chit-chat after hours.

Marshall gave the office one last look and then locked the door behind him. Life had been an adventure thus far, who knew what was in store for him next? Whatever it was, he just hoped it didn't involve Stewart. He'd had enough of him in one day to last a lifetime.

Chapter XXVII

The coach gradually slowed to a stop. A door creaked opened in the distance and shortly after, Alice heard a greeting to Brigid from an older female.

"Are you our newest recruit?" the lady inquired.

"Yes, Sister."

"Mother Mary Catherine," the woman replied. "It's a pleasure to meet you."

"Likewise," Brigid responded.

"If you have everything, then you can dismiss your driver, and we'll go meet the other members of the order."

"That sounds lovely, Mother Mary Catherine, but this isn't everything. Would you happen to have someone to assist Jeremiah in unloading the rest of my items? A strong male would be preferable."

A moment of silence ensued. "You do know we have a vow of poverty here, right?"

"That's exactly what my father asked me," said Brigid brightly. "I will assure you, just as I did my father, I am quite aware of that."

"Then explain the excess luggage, if you will."

"I will be happy to do that once everything is inside," said Brigid.

"Poverty, chastity, obedience. You would do well to remember those three words," uttered the sister.

A minute later, footsteps could be heard shuffling toward the coach. The farthest trunk from her, in which Marcus was concealed, scraped along the wood planking as it was shifted to the back deck of the vehicle.

It sounded as though it was a struggle for the second person bearing his portion of the load. Alice was concerned that whoever was helping Jeremiah might suffer a stroke, trying to lift something so heavy.

Thankfully, the two men finished that task and were back to the coach just a few minutes later. The trunk with Daisy and Abraham was lighter, so it took less time for them to return to grab the trunk that she and Josiah occupied.

She held tightly to the baby as they were jostled around. Alice prayed to The Blessed Mother to intercede on their behalf for safety as the trunk was set inside a building.

"Thank you for your assistance, Jeremiah," said Brigid sincerely. "I know you must get back to the house immediately. Please let my family know that I've arrived safe and sound. I appreciate all your help."

"Been a pleasure, miss," answered the man.

"Mother Mary Catherine, may I have a minute alone with you?"

"This is highly unusual, Miss McGinnis. What exactly is going on here?"

"Unusual may be an understatement, Mother." The straps on the trunk furthest from Alice were undone. Then the next one and finally the one in which she was hidden.

With a sense of relief, she felt the clothing above her being removed from the trunk. Peeking out, she saw Marcus peering down at her. She handed Josiah to him and then unfolded herself and stepped out of the container. Alice guessed that the wooden floor on which she stood was the entryway of the Sisters of Mercy convent.

A gasp came from the bespectacled stick-thin woman in full habit. She stalked to the windows and shut the curtains and turned to Brigid. "What in the name of the good Lord have you brought here?" she demanded to know. "Have you come to our order under duplicitous terms?"

"No, Mother Mary Catherine." Brigid stood tall, or as tall as she could, considering her stature. "My intentions are completely honorable, let me assure you. These people, who stand before you, need safe passage out of Georgia. I had them accompany me with the hope that they could find refuge here for a few days. One of the children is suffering from an ailment of the lungs. It may be serious."

"Are you telling me these people are runaway slaves?" asked the sister, lowering her voice.

"They are," admitted Brigid. "But, if you were to hear their story, I know you would feel a sense of compassion for the plight they've endured, just as I have."

"No need to waste your breath, Miss McGinnis. I know exactly how to deal with them."

Alice, Brigid, Marcus and Daisy stood motionless as they waited to hear the mother superior expound on her remarks. The lady in question perused the four of them, then, making the Sign of the Cross, called for Sister Mary Peter to come to the entryway.

When the younger sister walked into the area, she was introduced as Mother Mary Catherine's assistant. "Sister Mary Peter, as you can see, we have guests. This young lady is..." she paused, glancing toward Alice, and turned to Brigid for an answer.

"That's Alice, Mother Superior, and the infant is her son Josiah."

"Nice to meet you, Alice," said the mother superior with a nod.

"And you, as well, ma'am," replied Alice.

"Whom do we have here?"

"My name is Marcus. Miz Alice's brother. And this be my woman Daisy and our son Abraham."

"Abraham, say you? That's a fine name. Let's pray he will grow up to be as honorable a man as our president, Mr. Abraham Lincoln."

"That's the fellow he's named for," noted Marcus proudly.

"Mr. Marcus, you said Daisy is your woman. Is she not your wife?"

"No, ma'am," he said with a note of shame in his voice. "Our master never gave us permission to jump the broom."

"That can be remedied easily enough. We've a priest close by and plenty of sisters to act as witnesses. It won't do for Abraham's paternity to be in question."

Daisy's face lit up. "Thank you, ma'am," she said shyly.

"It's my pleasure — and I presume the Lord will delight in seeing you legally wed as well."

She turned to Sister Mary Peter. "Get a couple of rooms aired out for our guests. They'll be with us until the baby is ready to travel again. Send a message to the stationmaster at the next stop that we have passengers who will be ready for pick-up in a week or two."

"Yes, Mother Superior."

"Alice, Sister Mary Peter will take charge of your

group while you are on our premises. You have my word that she can be trusted. After all, she took her name in honor of our Blessed Mother, who along with her husband, Saint Joseph, and son, Jesus, was a fugitive herself. Saint Peter is the patron saint of slaves. You'll be in good hands with her."

Instinctively, Alice dropped to her knees, made the Sign of the Cross, and started praying. "*Ave Maria, gratia plena, Dominus tecum. Benedicta tu in mulieribus, et benedictus fructus ventris tui, Iesus. Sancta Maria, Mater Dei, ora pro nobis peccatoribus, nunc, et in hora mortis nostrae. Amen.*"

Brigid looked at her as if she'd grown two heads.

Doesn't she know that Negroes can be Catholic?

"Sister Mary Peter, would you be kind enough to show our guests where they may freshen up?"

"Yes, Mother Superior."

"We've a stock of clothing in the back room. There should be something to fit each of you so you can discard the clothing you're wearing. Finding the proper fit may be a challenge, Marcus, given your size."

The three young adults each thanked the older sister and then followed behind Sister Mary Peter as she headed towards the living quarters of the convent. Alice let the group get ahead of her and stepped into the shadows. She knew it was wrong to eavesdrop, but she felt it necessary to hear the conversation between Brigid and the mother superior.

"Thank you, young lady, for bringing this precious cargo safely to us," said the woman.

"You're...welcome, Mother Superior," Brigid stammered out.

"Are you an experienced conductor, or is this your

maiden voyage, my dear?"

"I beg your pardon?"

After a slight pause, the sister inquired, "How did you come upon these people that you brought here today?"

"I found Alice and her baby in the barn on our property one night. She led me to her brother and his family, who were hiding in our root cellar. Alice implored me not to turn them over to the authorities. Her master is the father of her baby, and he wanted her to dispose of it before it was born. She couldn't bring herself to punish the child for the sins of its father."

"I see," said Mother Mary Catherine. "Tell me why you brought them here with you."

"Of course, Mother," said Brigid. "I imagine you were aware that I would be joining the Sisters of Mercy before I even knew. By chance, my father arrived home from Virginia the same night I encountered Alice. He informed me that he had chosen an order for me, and I would be leaving our house less than a day later to take my place here. It was all in God's timing, as they say, because it proved to be the ideal moment to get them off our property. I took our driver Jeremiah into my confidences, and he helped me transport these people to your door."

"Do you intend to make your vows with us, Miss McGinnis?" the sister asked.

"That *is* my father's intention and, until two weeks ago, that was my intention as well. Now, I'm not so sure. Something happened that has caused me to have other considerations."

"Would that be something or someone?" Mother Mary Catherine asked.

"There is a time of discernment here, is there not?"

"Of course, my dear. You may spend up to twelve months as a postulant. If, after that time, you decide to continue the process, you will be admitted as a novitiate."

Alice's eyebrows shot up. *The prim Miss Brigid has a beau? Who'd have guessed?*

Chapter XXVIII

With everything that had gone on in the last week or so, Marshall would be late reaching his posting in Little Rock. Assisting Stewart had put him behind two days and, on top of that, he'd been instructed to bring correspondence to a Confederate troop stationed just outside of Cartersville on his way.

Anyone who could read a map knew that Cartersville was due north of Dallas. Seeing that he was supposed to be traveling west to Arkansas, it was a detour, to say the least. *There must be someone else who could act as a delivery boy. But who am I to question the inner workings of the Confederate Army?*

The folks in Little Rock were appraised via telegram of his altered route, so at least they wouldn't consider him absent without leave when he didn't arrive on the assigned day.

Who knew what he'd find when he got there? Little Rock had been captured by Union forces last year. It hadn't been that difficult of an endeavor. Martial law, the draft, and high taxes had led to a decline in enthusiasm for the Confederate cause amongst the citizens of the state capital.

A man named Isaac Murphy established a new Arkansan government not more than a month ago, but he and his followers struggled to gain recognition from the Union authorities as to their legitimacy because President Lincoln and his cabinet members were battling over which terms should be imposed on states that had seceded from the Union.

With Little Rock and the nearby Fort Smith under Union control, many of the Union forces had been withdrawn and sent to reinforce units east of the Mississippi. With no army backing him, Murphy's government was powerless in areas beyond the reach of the Union garrisons in the Arkansas River Valley.

Marshall was commissioned to train Confederate troops in hand-to-hand combat for the guerilla warfare that was being conducted in the virtual no man's land north of the Arkansas River.

Five weeks ago, the Confederate Army had notched a victory against the Union forces during the Camden Expedition. Two federal units were supposed to converge in the Red River Valley and strike into Texas, but they missed their mark. U.S. Brigadier General Frederick Steele's column suffered severe losses in a series of battles — Battle of Mark's Mills, Battle of Poison Spring and the Battle of Jenkins' Ferry — led by CSA Major General Sterling Price and Lieutenant General E. Kirby Smith.

With a renewed sense of optimism, Brigadier General Joseph O. Shelby and his cavalry brigade were dispatched to northeast Arkansas and began recruiting again. New recruits meant more training for Marshall. Men who'd either deserted or had been separated from their previous commands were returning to Confederate command and would be under his leadership.

So many soldiers poured into the area that four new Arkansas Mounted Infantry units were formed and dispatched to northeast Arkansas. With the strengthening of forces in the area, vital Union lines of communication along the Arkansas River were seriously threatened.

That was the news he'd been apprised of as of yesterday, but things changed quickly on the battlefront. First things first, though, he needed to find that regiment in Cartersville and deliver his missive.

Traveling the countryside at night wouldn't have been his first choice, but he needed to make up for the time he'd lost dealing with Stewart. With just a couple miles to go, he'd be there before midnight.

A noise came to his ears, causing him to bring Maximus to a halt. As it grew louder, Marshall realized that a vehicle of some sort was racing in his direction. To be on the safe side, he turned the horse into the woods that ran alongside the road.

He tethered Maximus near a patch of pine trees so he wouldn't be visible from the road. Then he positioned himself behind the trunk of an overgrown oak and waited for the conveyance to drive past him.

Just as it approached, Marshall took a glance over his shoulder and spotted a lone rider on a horse galloping towards Cartersville. Their two paths would intersect just in front of where he was hiding. *This could get interesting.*

Chapter XXIX

A persistent knocking drew Alice out of her room. Brigid was a step ahead of her and scurried into the entryway to answer the door before the noise woke the babies.

Alice found herself once again lurking in the shadows so that she could keep an eye on Brigid, with whom she was developing a friendship. A person appearing on the doorstep of the convent this time of night could only mean bad news.

Daisy must have figured the same thing. She sidled up behind Alice, and the two of them held their breath as they waited to hear the exchange.

The door creaked on its hinges as it was swung open.

"So, if it isn't Miss Brigid, or should I say, Sister Brigid?" Both she and Daisy stiffened with fear. The voice was unmistakable. It was Stewart.

"Go get Marcus," she frantically whispered to the frightened girl behind her.

Daisy nodded and silently retreated down the hall toward the sleeping quarters.

"Didn't I just see you walking around in layman's clothes this spring? Who'd have thought I'd run across you in little ol' Cartersville."

"The same can be said of you," replied Brigid coldly. "But it is still Miss Brigid. I've just started my studies. What business do you have here?"

"That's a good question, *Miss* Brigid, so I'll be succinct. I've got some property that's gone missing."

Alice's ears started to ring. She shook her head to

swish away the lightheadedness and resumed listening.

"I was out of town on business, and circumstances beyond my control delayed my return to our plantation. Upon my arrival, I was apprised of the situation. Immediately, I rounded up the bloodhounds and started tracking. The trail may have been a bit cold, but, interestingly enough, the dogs led me to your old place."

Brigid made no reply.

"Lo and behold, from there, I was led to this building and, consequently, to you."

"If you lay a hand on me, Stewart, so help me, I'll scream," said Brigid icily.

"You're not going to want to do that," Stewart replied. The threat in his voice caused Alice to shiver.

"I'd like you to step outside so we can talk."

"I have nothing to discuss with you," Brigid replied.

"Actually, I think you do," said Stewart. "If there's one thing the sisters taught well at Locust Grove Academy, it was mathematics. I can put two and two together. Let me lay this out for you. I own a plantation that runs on slave labor. The men, women and children living on that piece of land are my legal property. Every so often, one or two of them will get it in their head that they have the right to be free and will fashion a plan to escape."

"That's your business; it has nothing to do with me."

"I'm not so sure about that, Brigid. As I told you earlier, the bloodhounds tracked the scent of my escaped slaves to your father's house. I know the man has been in attendance with President Davis for the last several months. Your poor mother has gone mad since she lost her child — or since you took his life, if what I've heard is true."

Alice's eyes widened. There was much more to this young lady than she knew.

"That is a lie, and you know it," Brigid spat out.

"Regardless, you *do* run the household in your father's absence, do you not?"

Silence hung in the air.

"I'll take that as a yes. Being part of a slave patrol isn't as easy as it was back in the day. I doubt that darkies are getting any smarter, but the hearts and heads of the do-gooders are getting softer. Seems they've developed a system for assisting the fugitives in their flight. Some call it the Underground Railroad. I trust you've heard of it?"

After a beat, he continued, "Apparently, some of the houses on this network are used without the owner's permission. Your father is above reproach — I would never question his loyalty, being a slave owner himself."

I knew it! Alice gritted her teeth together.

"Seeing you're such a good Catholic girl and would never break the law, I was willing to give you the benefit of the doubt when I arrived there yesterday."

Alice wished she dare glance around the corner to see Brigid's reaction. She wondered what was going through her head.

"Have I caught you off guard, Brigid? You knew your papa owned the household help, did you not? We were at auction together when he purchased a handmaid for your birthday less than two years ago. I personally inspected her myself, so I knew she would be docile and cooperative — the perfect fit for a fine young lady like yourself."

That evil snake! A shiver ran down Alice's spine.

"Now that I think of it, you probably didn't know about your father's side business. Banking is a solid trade but not quite lucrative enough to keep his family living in the fashion they had come to enjoy over the years. Being the respectable church-goer that Mr. McGinnis is, he kept those affairs between himself and a few fellow businessmen, including my sire. Your father really didn't want to sully his reputation by announcing to the world that he was involved in such sordid dealings. So, he threatened a whipping to any of the slaves in your household who let on that they were anything other than hired help. As I was building my resume back then, I was more than happy to hone my thrashing skills on anyone who got out of line."

The man was not bluffing. Alice had seen his handiwork for herself.

"Speaking of whipping, that brings me back to the current situation with which we're dealing. I won't sugarcoat this, Brigid. My presumption — and I would put money on this that I'm correct — is that you've somehow been coerced into siding with the bleeding-heart abolitionists. While your father has been away on business, you've opened your home to runaway slaves," Stewart said accusingly.

"If it had been anyone else's property, I doubt that I'd be chasing these animals hither and yon, but this is personal. I need to make sure we get them back so we can use them as an example to discourage other runaways. It will be quite the spectacle for their fellow slaves to see me whip those escapees within an inch of their lives. Of course, it isn't always easy judging how much a human body can take. Occasionally I get a bit overzealous."

The reality of Stewart's words hit Alice like a bucketful of icy spring water.

"Did I mention, too, that we follow the dictates of the Fugitive Act of 1850? As slave patrollers, we are allowed to use our own good judgment to levy punishment upon those citizens who interfere with the capture of slaves. It's an unfortunate task, but someone needs to do it."

"Stewart, I have no idea what you're talking about, but even if your suppositions were true, and the people you are searching for were on these premises, this property belongs to the Catholic Church — it's a sanctuary."

"I wouldn't dare broach such sacred territory," said Stewart patronizingly. "But we have developed ways to smoke animals out."

"You wouldn't dare burn down a convent. Have you no consideration for your soul?" exclaimed Brigid. "You would be risking the lives of all the women religious here."

"That's what we refer to as collateral damage."

Alice's heart pounded uncontrollably. *Stewart has always been a tyrant, but now he's gone completely mad.*

"You know, Brigid, now that I think about it... Endangering one's soul is a precarious proposition, so how about I just turn around, depart from this city, and leave well enough alone?"

Alice wasn't fooled by the conciliatory tone.

"I'm a man who is willing to compromise if the situation warrants such an action. To be honest, the lives of those slaves mean nothing to me. But I suspect, with your tenderhearted nature, they have some significance for you."

He paused. "I will let them escape Scot-free and make sure you are free from incrimination on one condition – that you accompany me back to my plantation and take my hand in marriage."

"Are you jesting?" Brigid asked incredulously. "What in God's name would make you put forth such an offer, and why on earth would I even consider such a thing?"

"It's a business transaction, Brigid. My parents had always desired to see me wed so the family name could be passed down to my offspring. You're from an upstanding family, and, seeing how you've matured through the years, I'd say you're probably the best catch in our county."

"I'm not a horse to be sold at auction and bred," Brigid shot back with indignation.

"That's an interesting analogy," said Stewart. "Actually, you do remind me of a filly in need of a powerful man to break her. Brigid, you can be headstrong and try to resist me, but the consequences won't be pretty, let me assure you. It's your choice now – you either come along with me nice and sweet-like, or I set to work with my original plan. You have ten seconds to decide."

Chapter XXX

A male and female sat next to each other on the seat of the wagon. Marshall recognized the man in a heartbeat. It was Stewart.

Glancing again at the other person, he did a double-take. It was a religious sister. And a young one at that. *What in God's name is Stewart up to?*

From what he knew of the scoundrel, seeing any woman in Stewart's grip made his hackles rise. While the young lady appeared to be accompanying him of her own volition, she put as much space between herself and him as she could without falling off the seat.

From his vantage point, he watched as the approaching horse, which he could now clearly see was ridden by a Union soldier, drew near and came to a dead stop in front of the vehicle. The scene unfolded before him. He was prepared to step in, if necessary, but he needed to understand the essence of their exchange before he did anything.

The young lady, upon seeing the soldier, let out a gasp. Stewart spun his head towards her, just as her hand flew up and covered her mouth. Her eyes were as wide as saucers.

He eyed her up suspiciously before turning back to the soldier. "What's the matter, Sergeant? You lose track of your Uncle Sam?"

"I should say not. As a matter of fact, he and Honest Abe got me on a mission tonight. Looking for Reb stragglers. It seems to me I've found one."

"As you can see, officer, I wear no uniform. I'm just a civilian minding my own business."

"And what business would that be that involves traveling with a woman of the cloth unescorted in the middle of the night?"

The sister clutched the wooden bench as though she thought to propel herself from it. Noticing that, Stewart's eyes went back and forth between her and the soldier. Realization dawned on his face.

"Well, isn't this a fine kettle of fish? If I'm not mistaken, you two have met before. Your pious façade is starting to tarnish, Brigid."

Brigid? Was this Brigid McGinnis, daughter of John Thaddeus McGinnis, Secretary of the Interior of the Confederate States of America? The McGinnis house was where he'd last seen Alice. *What were the odds that he'd encounter anyone from that family in the middle of the night along some dusty country road?*

"Is this man the conductor you have been working with to steal my property? Or, perhaps, you know each other on a more intimate basis."

"How dare you say something so scandalous, Stewart," Brigid shot back.

So, the two of them are on a first-name basis. Marshall couldn't fathom why she and Stewart were traveling together, particularly seeing that she was a woman of the cloth. *Or was she?*

"The lady doth protest too much, methinks," said Stewart. "Wouldn't that be something if, not only did I track down my property tonight, but, in the process, I found the abolitionist who escorted them *and* a federal soldier who's aiding and abetting her? This would be one for the books."

Hearing the word "property," Marshall's breath caught in his throat. Was Stewart referring to Alice?

At that moment, Brigid pushed herself down from the wagon. She hit the ground, but the echo of the hammer of a gun being clicked into place stopped her dead in her tracks. Both she and the soldier pivoted their heads towards Stewart. The derringer in his hand glinted in the moonlight.

"I wouldn't do that if I were you, Brigid. You sold your soul to me tonight, and the only way you're getting out of it is if some tragedy would befall you."

Stewart edged towards the passenger side of the vehicle and then bounded down to ground level. Keeping the derringer in his right hand, he bent down and grabbed Brigid's upper arm. Tugging her to her feet, he proceeded to drag her in front of the horses. The soldier's hand hovered above his holster.

"Don't even think about it, Yank."

Pulling Brigid in close, Stewart pressed the barrel of his gun to her right temple. "You make one wrong move, and she's gone. This one's a tasty-looking morsel, but there are plenty of young women who'd come swimming around, given the right bait. Besides, if she dies, then she reneges on our agreement, and I get my property back from the sisters. I doubt if any of them would trade their lives for a bunch of darkies, like this sanctimonious little lady did."

Marshall absorbed every word that the man said. Had this girl given up her freedom in exchange for Alice's liberty? *That's remarkable.*

Stewart pointed to the other man. "I want you to ease that gun out of the holster and toss it into the ditch."

Reluctantly, the soldier did as he was told. Stewart

then released his grip on Brigid's arm and yanked her veil off. He interlaced his fingers in her hair and snapped her head back. "How about we give your beau a little entertainment before he heads off to his eternal reward?"

His lips brushed Brigid's cheek.

"No," she screamed, wrenching her head back as far from him as she could.

Movement coming from the underside of the wagon caught Marshall's eye. A large, dark figure crept from behind the vehicle and stealthily approached Stewart and Brigid. In a flash, the man grabbed Stewart's right arm and twisted it behind his back.

A gunshot sounded. The soldier sprinted to Brigid. Meanwhile, the behemoth of a man wrapped his free arm around Stewart's neck. He had him in the crook of his elbow and forced the appendage down in one quick motion. A horrendous sound reverberated through the still night air — the sound of Stewart's neck-snapping. He keeled over, dead.

Brigid's eyes rolled up, and her face drained of all color. The soldier was there in time to catch her before she followed Stewart to the ground. He swept her up into his arms and assessed her injuries.

He then turned to the black man. The giant staggered backward three steps and fell to the ground, clutching his thigh.

Freeing herself from the soldier's grip, Brigid dropped to the ground and ran towards the injured man. She fell to her knees before him.

Both Brigid and Marshall had the revelation at the same time. *It was Marcus.*

Chapter XXXI

Alice was beside herself with worry. It was bad enough that Stewart had taken Brigid from the convent, but Marcus had set out after them. She'd spent the last two hours pacing the wooden floor in the convent entryway. And she was on her seventh recitation of the Rosary.

By now, the sisters were aware of the situation. Mother Mary Catherine was wearing her rosary beads thin alongside her.

Hearing a wagon pull up, Alice ran to the door. Throwing caution to the wind, she yanked the portal open. Brigid and a man in a Union military uniform were assisting Marcus from the vehicle.

Pulling her skirt up a bit, she ran toward the road.

"Marcus!" She came to a dead halt. There was blood on his trousers. It appeared that he'd taken a gunshot to the leg.

Alice glanced back toward the convent. The sisters were gathered in the entryway, peeking around the mother superior like a brood of frightened chickens.

"Praise God, you're back," said Sister Mary Catherine, stepping outside. Peering closer, she noticed the blood on Brigid's habit. "Dear Lord, are you all right?

The girl nodded. Sister grabbed Brigid's hands. "You can't imagine how many prayers have been said for your well-being since we discovered you missing." The other women, who'd flooded out of the building, bobbed their veiled heads in agreement.

Looking beyond Brigid, Mother Mary Catherine noticed Marcus leaning on the Union officer for support as they started up the walk. She directed Brigid towards the other sisters and turned her attention to the two men. Her face showed concern when she saw Marcus.

"Let's get him into the convent immediately, Sergeant. We can make our introductions once we're inside."

The soldier followed the woman's command. When they were all in the building, the mother superior assisted Marcus to his sleeping quarters. She then instructed one of the postulants to fetch Sister Mary Phillip, who was trained as a nurse.

After Marcus was settled in his room, Mother Mary Catherine returned to the entryway. Assured that her loved one was in capable hands, Alice soon followed. As ill at ease she felt with her new habit of listening in on conversations, she needed to find out what had gone on.

Sister addressed Brigid and the man. "You know each other, I assume."

"Yes, ma'am," said the soldier.

Alice's eyebrows shot up. *Brigid knows a Union soldier? I assume her father isn't aware of that.*

"Would this by any chance be the someone who has caused you to reconsider taking religious vows, Miss McGinnis?"

What? Alice closed her gaping jaw.

With no words spoken, she tried to imagine the looks being exchanged between the young man and the young lady. Finally, Brigid spoke up.

"If you wouldn't mind, Mother Mary Catherine, may I have a moment alone with the gentleman?"

Chapter XXXII

As tempting as it was, Marshall couldn't leave Stewart's body to be eaten by the wolves. When morning came, he'd stop by the sheriff's department — assuming a community the size of Cartersville had one — and report that he'd spotted the body when he was coming into town.

Of course, there'd be no mention of actually seeing the man come to his demise. He wasn't sure what precipitated the incident, but he was positive that Marcus had just cause for taking that man's life.

After the confrontation, Marshall had discretely followed the wagon transporting Marcus into Cartersville. Part of him wanted to make sure that the man got back into town safely, and the other part was hoping to catch a glimpse of Alice. Undoubtedly, they were hiding in the same spot.

When they'd come closer to town, a steeple loomed over on the horizon. The vehicle rumbled in that direction and, in due time, had pulled up in front of a church. A separate building was on the same grounds. He made out the words "Sisters of Mercy" chiseled into a stone sign situated on the corner of the lot.

Despite the late hour, the building was ablaze. Perhaps they'd known of Marcus' mission and were awaiting his return? Marshall found a spot to secure his horse and position himself to keep the building in his sightline.

Brigid and the Union soldier had helped Marcus down from the wagon. The girl then made her way slowly toward the building. The soldier put his arm around the slave, and they hobbled after her.

Before any of them made it to the door, the portal swung open. A young woman ran toward Marcus.

The light from the building illuminated a sister inside the entryway, whom Marshall assumed was the mother superior. Peeking behind her were several other sisters, worry engraved upon every visage.

From his position, Marshall couldn't hear the words going back and forth, but the interactions were clear. As was evidenced by their level of concern, the sisters knew both Marcus and Brigid and were greatly relieved to see them.

The injured man was helped into the convent. With everyone crowded in the candlelit hallway, he had been able to make out all of the faces. The young woman in lay clothing was clearly visible.

It was Alice. He'd never been so relieved in his life. How she ended up in Cartersville, of all places, was beyond him. But, seeing that God sought to bring them this close together again, Marshall felt it was his duty to speak to her. He settled into the shadows, waiting until the soldier left the grounds so he could go to the convent himself.

In the meantime, he took in what he could from his position. Through the open window, he saw the mother superior directing a sister to move Marcus to another part of the building. Perhaps they had someone trained in medicine in their order. *As smart and well-read as Alice is, maybe she can help him.*

Moments later, the older woman returned to the entryway. She addressed the soldier and the young lady. From what he could tell, the couple seemed a bit uncomfortable.

After a few more words were exchanged, the mother superior vacated the area, and the couple was alone.

Marshall didn't want to intrude on their meeting, but he had to keep an eye on the situation so he'd know when the coast was clear, and he could seek out Alice.

With the sister gone, the young girl pivoted toward the man, crossed her arms and an inquisition began. Watching the soldier weather the storm of questions, Marshall was glad that he wasn't in the line of fire.

As the man answered each question, various emotions crossed Brigid's face. When her countenance brightened with happiness, it appeared that things were turning in a positive direction for the defendant.

That suspicion was confirmed when the man stepped toward the young lady and engulfed her in his arms. His declaration made her eyes light up. After bestowing a smile on her, the man cupped her chin in his hand.

Looks like they've come to an agreement. The man then took control of the conversation. He'd just pulled Brigid back into his arms when the mother superior made an untimely reappearance.

After a brief private exchange with the older woman, the man stepped back to Brigid. He seemed to be pouring his heart out to her. The look on his face was so loving and sincere that Marshall thought for an instance that he might be on the verge of proposing.

As discourteous as it was, he couldn't tear his eyes away from the scene. Maybe he'd pick up a tip for when it was his turn to ask for a girl's hand in marriage. God willing, it would be Alice. He said a quick prayer to St. Edwin — his namesake and patron saint — asking for his intercessory prayers in the matter.

When the man picked the young lady up and swirled her around, Marshall thought maybe it actually had been a proposal, as unconventional as it may have appeared. Once the girl's feet were back on the floor, she got another hug from the soldier and a chaste kiss on her forehead.

The man broke away from Brigid and addressed the mother superior. He reached in his pocket and produced a stack of Greenbacks which he proceeded to press into the lady's hand.

Well, I've seen just about everything. Was that man bribing a sister?

With one last word to his intended, the man crossed the threshold and made his way outside the building. He hadn't gone more than three steps when the young lady threw herself out the door and caught up with him.

The soldier turned around. Brigid grabbed him by the lapels and firmly planted a kiss on his lips. When they broke away from each other, the man waved and jauntily headed to his horse, whistling as he went. The girl wrapped her arms around herself and skipped back into the building.

Marshall couldn't help but give a wry smile. Maybe someday that'd be him and Alice. But, before that could happen, they'd need to have a heart-to-heart chat. Even though Stewart was gone, it was imperative that he discern the true depth of that man's relationship with her.

Chapter XXXIII

Brigid practically floated back into the building. Alice's eyes widened. *That conversation must have gone well.* She grinned as the smitten young lady glided off to her sleeping chambers.

Just as Alice was preparing to bolt the entryway door, a knock sounded. Assuming it was the Union sergeant returning, she swung the door open expectantly.

Taking a step back, she choked out, "Marshall? What on earth are you doing here?"

"Just happened to be going through town. I realize it's after midnight, but I took a chance that you may still be up."

His statement was so matter-of-fact that she had to take a moment to consider if it could possibly be true.

"You're jesting, right?"

A broad smile came to his face. Alice eyed him curiously. She wasn't accustomed to lighthearted teasing.

Regardless, she couldn't imagine what actually had brought him to the door of the convent – especially seeing that Union soldiers were in the area. Personally, she'd welcomed the sight of the Northern Army, but she didn't figure that he'd be too thrilled about the prospect.

As happy as she was to see Marshall standing before her, it was somewhat troubling as well. If he tracked her down so easily, Stewart's men could as well. Once the fate of their ringleader was discovered, they'd be on the warpath. And, undoubtedly, she'd be their primary target.

"How on earth did you ever find me?" she blurted out.

"The good Lord led me here, Miss Alice," Marshall replied.

"Elaborate on that assertion, if you would."

"As you are aware, when I brought you to the McGinnis house, I was not informed of your next destination. Of course, you may not have known that at the time either."

That was true. The original plan that she'd laid out called for the fugitives to flee due north through Tennessee into Kentucky. Yet, here they were, closer to the border of Alabama than Tennessee.

"My next assignment, as you may recall, is in Little Rock. I was to report to duty this coming Monday. Providentially, my plans were rearranged thanks to an old friend of yours."

Alice searched her memory, trying to guess to whom he referred. Other than her family, the other house slaves at Pecan Hall, and, as of late, Brigid, she couldn't honestly say that she had any friends.

Seeing her questioning look, Marshall filled her in.

"Stewart."

"Stewart," she echoed incredulously. *That man is the last person on earth I'd consider a friend.*

"He came to my office earlier this week in search of you."

Clutching the front of her dress, Alice took a step back. "I never intended for you to get involved in this, Marshall."

"Perhaps not, but I am," he replied evenly. "Young Mr. Williams was intent on enlisting the help of the Confederate Army to apprehend some runaway slaves from Pecan Hall."

"You actually agreed to help him?" Alice asked indignantly.

"Only as a ruse, to lead him astray from your hiding spot."

Alice could have cried in relief. She hadn't wanted to think the worst of Marshall, but in truth, she barely knew him. Every time she glanced at him, though, her rational mind went astray, leaving just her heart to do all the thinking.

Marshall continued. "He and I searched Dallas side by side for an entire day searching for you. In that timeframe, I got to know him to a degree."

Eyes narrowing, Alice waited to see where this disclosure would lead.

"As unusual as the circumstances were, he seemed to genuinely care about you."

A feeling of disgust ran through her. *If that was the case, he had an odd way of showing it.*

"Matter of fact, he was quite taken with you. From the way he put it, it sounded as though the feeling was mutual."

Bile rose to Alice's throat. "Stewart was delusional if he thought that I had any feelings towards him other than revulsion. And if you would take his word over mine, you're no better than he is."

Hands shaking, she grabbed the edge of the convent door and slammed it soundly in Marshall's face.

Chapter XXXIV

Marshall swung the door back open and strode across the hallway to grab the hand of the hastily retreating young woman.

"Not so fast, little lady."

"Let me go," she ground out, doing her best to keep her voice low.

"Never," he replied.

Putting his other arm around her back, he escorted Alice towards the door. She dug her heels into the wood planks but couldn't stop his momentum.

"Remember what I said before?" he inquired. "We can do this the easy way or the hard way."

"Fine," she spat, yanking her hand from his and jamming her arms across her chest. "I'll follow you."

"Let's have me follow you, why don't we? That lessens the chances of the back of my head getting nipped by the closing door as you lock me out of the convent."

Giving in, Alice stepped over the threshold and into the cool night air.

"How about we go for a nice stroll and chat?" he suggested.

"If we must."

He had to get to the bottom of this story. Diving in headfirst, he started his line of questioning. "You say you had no feelings for Stewart, but you did bear his child."

"Against my will!" she sputtered out.

"That's not the way Stewart made it sound."

Alice drew her hand back and slapped Marshall soundly across the face.

"How dare you say something so vile!"

He rubbed his cheek to lessen the sting. For a petite thing, she packed a pretty good punch.

Had Stewart's warped thinking infected his own thoughts? The vision of Alice in that miscreant's arms made him grit his teeth. *Maybe my own jealously is getting the best of me.*

Pinning Alice's arms to her side to keep from getting clocked again, Marshall picked up where he'd left off, this time softening his line of attack.

"You say you were with him against your will. Did he beat you into submission?"

She looked at him uneasily. "I was never whipped or abused in any such a fashion."

Marshall wasn't sure what to make of her confession. "Then you went willingly into his arms?" His heart ached as he waited for her answer.

"Trust me. I wanted nothing to do with that man." She blinked hard, tears threatening to spill from her eyes.

While most young women could bring on the waterworks to connive a man or get themselves out of trouble, he knew in his heart that Alice was not one to manufacture such an artifice.

"If there was no threat of violence, then why would you go to him?"

"No threat of violence? I'd hardly say that. There was no threat to me because Stewart wasn't one to dally with damaged goods. But he had no issue beating the people that I cared about, including my own *maman*."

Realization dawned on Marshall. Before he could say anything to apologize for thinking the worst of her, she continued.

"I was a birthday gift to him the day he turned eighteen and officially reached manhood," she spat out. "Just as my mother had been gifted to his father when he became a so-called man."

She narrowed her eyes at Marshall and finished. "His grandfather bought my grandmother with the express idea of owning her body and soul. The men in that family are depraved."

With that, the tears cascaded down her cheeks. Marshall pulled her into his arms and gently rubbed her back as she wept. He felt like a heel for forcing her to share her darkest secret with him.

When the river was reduced to a trickle, he pulled back and gently wiped the trail of tears from her cheeks.

"I'm sorry," he stated simply. "Who am I to accuse you of anything? We haven't even known each other a month." His eyes dropped. "But hearing Stewart talk about you in such intimate terms, my mind became clouded with jealousy."

"Jealousy?" Alice couldn't hide the astonishment in her voice. "Stewart was my master. Regardless of what he led you to believe, I was his slave, not his paramour."

Voice choked with emotion, she continued, "And I always will be. Even if I'm fortunate enough to escape this godforsaken state, I'll never be free of him. Stewart is vindictive and as wicked as Satan himself. He'll hunt me down until the day I die."

Marshall's head snapped up. *Alice doesn't know that*

Stewart's dead.

"How could you possibly be jealous anyhow?" she questioned. "That's an emotion reserved for a man when he loves a woman — someone he hopes to marry someday."

A small sob escaped her throat. "I should be the one apologizing to you, Marshall. I tricked you into believing that I was something that I was not."

"As clever as you thought you were, *ma cherie*, I wasn't deceived."

Her eyes widened. "You weren't?"

"No. I knew that you were of African heritage the moment I laid eyes on you. But you know what? It didn't matter then, and it doesn't matter now. I fell head over heels for you that day, and nothing you can say or do will ever change the way I feel."

It took a second for the words to sink in. Tears sprang once again to Alice's eyes.

"I have to admit that I have feelings for you too, Marshall. But I can never be yours. Stewart would kill me before he'd allow such a thing to happen."

Marshall gathered her into his arms and whispered into her ear. "There's no need to worry about Stewart anymore. Thanks to Marcus, he's gone."

Chapter XXXV

Alice's head spun. Could it really be true that all the men in Williams' family were dead now? She should pray for their souls, but she just couldn't bring herself to do that yet. Her *maman* knew how to forgive, but she had a harder time of it. Someday, maybe, but not now.

For the moment, she would enjoy what little time she and Marshall had left together. The two of them walked hand in hand until dawn broke.

Those precious hours were spent discussing their plans for the immediate future. And what life may be like for them when the war was over. Marshall had his assignment to fulfill in Little Rock, and she needed to make sure that Marcus, Daisy and the little ones made it to Kentucky safely.

Their destination was Camp Nelson, located in Jessamine County. Ever since she'd read about the encampment when it was established two years ago, Alice had been determined to get herself and Marcus there. That was, however, before Daisy, Abraham and Josiah became part of the picture. But their arrival didn't deter her ambitions.

She could still clearly recall the first newspaper article that she'd read about the camp. *In December 1862, Major General Ambrose Burnside was assigned command of the newly formed Department of the Ohio by President Lincoln. The objective was to capture and hold eastern Tennessee and, in time, take Knoxville, a Confederate rail hub.*

In April 1863, a search committee was formed to identify a location that would allow the Department of the Ohio to consolidate troops and supplies in central Kentucky. A camp was established along the Lexington-Danville Turnpike, adjacent to the Kentucky River, near the cities of Nicholasville, Lexington and Richmond, along major lines of transportation.

Encompassing roughly four-thousand acres, Camp Nelson was organized around an eight-hundred-acre core upon which sat more than three-hundred tents and buildings that housed a recruitment center, quartermaster commissary depot, ordnance depot, prison, and a hospital. There were corrals and stables, a bakery, and steam-driven waterworks to pump water from the Kentucky River to a fifty-thousand-gallon reservoir. Eight earthen batteries protected the camp.

Camp Nelson was one of the largest of the eight Negro recruitment centers in Kentucky and the third-largest U.S. Colored Troops recruitment center in the nation. With restrictions on enlistments removed, the number of enlistees of African descent rose exponentially. Former slaves were emancipated through the act of enlistment in the Union army.

A good number of Negro men pouring into Camp Nelson were accompanied by their parents, wives and children, who were hoping to be granted freedom as well. Starting in 1861, under Union Army policy, freedom seekers who reached Union lines were considered contraband of war and granted freedom.

With that promise, Camp Nelson was the ideal place to run. Unfortunately, it hadn't worked out for everyone. Any slave who arrived unable to serve in the Union Army was expected to depart the camp and return to enslavement. Their families were expelled too.

Alice prayed that Marcus' leg would heal quickly and that he'd be found fit for service. If he wasn't accepted, they'd have to travel further north to a free state. The longer that they were on the road, the greater their chances of being apprehended.

After all she and Marshall had gone through, she was loath to be less than honest with him, but she knew he'd interfere with her plans if he discovered the extent of them. Once Marcus was up and about, the sisters would take him, Daisy and the babies to Camp Nelson, hidden in the compartment under their wagon's floorboards. She would not be accompanying them.

Even if Stewart was gone, his men weren't. Seeing that they could still be actively pursuing the fugitives from the Williams' estate, splitting from Marcus at this point was a more strategic plan. If the slave trackers had to follow one trail, she wanted it to be hers.

Chapter XXXVI

With the assurance that Alice had a plan sketched out to get her and the others to Camp Nelson, Marshall resumed his journey to Little Rock. Before he left, he had the chance to meet Brigid McGinnis and thank her for her role in helping the Pecan Hall fugitives escape.

It turned out that initially, she had no clue that her home was a stop on the Underground Railroad. But, when she stumbled upon Alice and her family, the girl's compassionate heart led her to allow them to stay on the property a few days until she was able to arrange their transport to the Sisters of Mercy convent in Cartersville.

By chance, he learned that Brigid was also heading to Little Rock. Albeit by train rather than horseback like him.

The interesting thing was, she was transferring to another Sisters of Mercy convent. It may have been just him, but the kiss she'd laid on that Union soldier was anything other than sisterly, to be blunt. *Was this just a ruse to keep her safe from Stewart's vigilante pals?*

That girl would have a lot of explaining to do if her father ever caught up with her. Lots of intrigue going on behind the scenes in this war nowadays.

No intrigue on his behalf, though. If luck was on his side, he'd be able to ride out the Little Rock assignment until the end of the hostilities.

While recent victories had brought a renewed sense

of optimism to some Confederates, Marshall had studied enough war history that he didn't share his compatriots' hopefulness. The path to victory for their side narrowed more as each day went by. Major General William Tecumseh Sherman of the Union Army was hell-bent on finishing this war off and, from what he knew of the West Point graduate, he'd go to any length to see that happen.

As for himself, he'd fill the instructor post outside Little Rock and keep training raw recruits until President Davis called it quits. Perhaps after that, he'd stop home and see how his parents made it through the war and then set out for Texas.

On May 20, 1862, President Lincoln had signed The Homestead Act of 1862. This decree gave citizens — or future citizens of the United States — up to 160 acres of public land. Other than a small registration fee, there was no charge.

The one catch was that the homesteader had to agree to live on the land and improve it. It was said that there were millions of acres up for grabs out west. *What would improve a piece of land more than setting up an attorney's office on it?*

This could be a winning proposition not only for himself embarking on his new career but for the untold number of pioneers who'd be looking to start new lives out there as well. Most men had just a rudimentary education. For a fee, he could help them wade through the paperwork required to stake their property claims.

Having been under the employ of the federal government for the last two years, he was a veritable expert in the field of paperwork. Duplicate, triplicate, whatever was asked of him, he could produce it.

For those fellows who didn't have what it took to improve their land, he had an ideal proposition. With the know-how to build, Marshall could construct a place on each parcel of land, sell it to the newcomers on an installment plan, and they'd pay the money back working the land.

That dream would have to wait for the time being. First, he had his duty to fulfill for ol' Jeff Davis.

Marshall had a knack for training soldiers, and he'd continue to do so. The only thing he'd have a hard time training was his conscience.

Whipping those young — and sometimes not-so-young — pups into shape to fight a losing battle gnawed at him. He would do his best to give them the skills that they needed to stay alive, but skirmishes were always unpredictable.

It bothered him that he may be sending these men off to be slaughtered. Whether it was the young guys, whose lives would be cut short in their prime, or the older men who had wives and children back home to support, he had a hard time justifying his role in the war.

To be truthful, the men with whom he'd be working weren't the pick of the litter. If they'd been left behind after the first round of enlistments three years ago, there'd been a good reason. Either they were too young and wet behind the ears, or they were past their prime.

One day he'd talk through this with a priest in Confession to ease his mind. But, until that time presented itself, he'd do as he was ordered. It didn't mean he had to like it, though.

At least there was one thing that he didn't have to worry about. The Sisters of Mercy assured him that

Alice was in good hands and that she'd be safe and sound at Camp Nelson before the week was through. That set his mind at ease.

Chapter XXXVII

Alice waved to the sisters as they departed with Marcus, Daisy and the babies hidden away in the wagon. It was a relief to see them off to Camp Nelson. She prayed that Daisy and the children would be able to stay there for the duration of the war.

Marcus would train with the Union Army. He was clever enough that it shouldn't take him long to learn how to handle a firearm. Not only that, a person of his stature should be able to best anyone man to man. His size made him a larger target, though, which was worrisome.

If the Union won — and from everything she'd been reading, it seemed that was the most likely outcome — then President Lincoln would free the slaves nationwide.

He'd issued the Emancipation Proclamation on January 1, 1863, as the third year of the conflict approached. The pronouncement declared that all persons held as slaves within the rebellious states were — and henceforward would be — free.

Despite this inclusive wording, the Emancipation Proclamation was limited. It only applied to states that had seceded from the United States, not the loyal border slave states, and it expressly exempted the Southern secessionist states that had already come under Union control. The freedom it promised depended upon the Federal Army winning the war.

Drawing in a shaky breath, Alice thought about her son. It grieved her to send Josiah with Marcus and

Daisy, but remaining with her would not only be unsafe for both of them but would only hamper her next mission. One that required going back to Dallas.

Thankfully, Daisy produced enough milk for both babies, so Josiah would be well-fed. She and Marcus loved him as much as they loved their own little Abraham, so he'd be nurtured and cherished. Her goal was to meet them at Camp Nelson as soon as she could.

First, though, she needed to secure the freedom of her younger sisters and brother.

It would not be an easy task. Mr. Williams' sister and her husband owned them. Their property, Rosewood Plantation, was several miles from Pecan Hall. When she got close to Marietta, someone should be able to direct her there.

The bigger issue may be getting herself in front of the children. She didn't even know if they were house slaves or field hands.

It had been more than eight years since they'd seen each other. She guessed that Gabrielle would recognize her despite her disguise. Juliette, probably not. As for Jacques, he was so young when they were separated that he might not even be aware that he had a third sister.

The endeavor wouldn't be easy, but if she could pull it off, it would be worth it. With Stewart's passing, this undertaking would be slightly less treacherous. He probably would have figured that she wouldn't leave her kin behind and, consequently, staked out Rosewood Plantation, awaiting her arrival. Hopefully, his henchmen were unaware of her ties to the place.

Over the last few weeks, she'd been formulating a plan. Even though Marshall had been able to see through her guise, she was certain that she could still pull the Caucasian ruse off.

She highly doubted that Mr. Williams' sister would recognize her. She'd hardly glanced at her the few times that they'd been in the same space together through the years.

All Alice needed to do was to create a plausible scenario to get herself inside the main house. She just wished that Marshall was with her this very moment. *He's probably much better at fabricating stories than I am.*

Chapter XXXVIII

What was the expression about the best-laid plans of mice and men?

Marshall hadn't been at the camp in Little Rock for more than a month when he got word via telegraph that the Cadet Rangers were being called up. He was to report to The Citadel by the first of August.

As he packed his bag, he recalled his last conversation with Alice when they had strolled through Cartersville.

"I'm sorry. I really am," he'd said contritely. "When Stewart told me of his obsession with you and bragged about your beauty and your accomplishments, I got mad with jealously. He was so convincing. I was suckered into believing him."

"My beauty and accomplishments? He'd uttered no such words to me," she'd said in disbelief. "If he'd truly harbored feelings for me, why was it that he wanted nothing to do with the baby?"

"What do you mean by that?"

"He'd presented the means for the child to be disposed of when I was well into the pregnancy."

"Disposed of? How in the world did he plan to do that?"

"I won't go into details, but there are ways," she'd responded. "But I refused to give my son a death sentence in atonement for the sins of his father. Josiah is an innocent victim in all this."

"I know he is. Regardless of his sire, the child

deserves just as much a chance for life, liberty and the pursuit of happiness as the rest of us."

Marshall had stared into Alice's warm brown eyes. "Then you forgive me for letting Stewart make me think the worst of you?"

She'd looked back at him intently as though she could read his soul.

"You're forgiven."

"Thank you, princess."

Alice gasped. "Why did you call me that?"

"It just seemed like the natural way to address you."

She eyed him warily.

"I meant no disrespect," he added hastily.

"Have you ever heard anyone refer to me in such a manner?" she asked.

Marshall thought for a moment. Then it occurred to him. "Ugh. Now I know why that upset you. Stewart used that term once when he talked of you."

"He knew?"

Alice immediately clapped her hands over her lips as if trying to take the words back.

"Knew what?"

Her hands fell back to her side. "Nothing. Forget I said anything."

Respecting her wishes, Marshall had dropped the topic, but it did make him wonder. Was the tale that Stewart had relayed to him true? Was Alice really of royal stock?

Bringing his mind back to the present, he pondered his next assignment. While he had managed for the most part to steer clear of the warfront for the last two years, it sounded as though his fellow Cadet Rangers back in South Carolina had been kept busy. They actively participated in several engagements and campaigns in defense of Charleston and the state as a whole.

The regimental colors of the South Carolina Corps of Cadets now carried four battle streamers. The first commemorated the Star of the West, January 9, 1861, then Wappoo Cut, November, 1861, James Island, June of 1862, and the Charleston campaign waged from July to October, 1863.

His friend and classmate, Cadet Ranger G. A. McDowell of the 6th South Carolina, had kept him abreast of the news via letters here and there. That was until his life was cut short in Gettysburg last year.

McDowell wasn't the first classmate of his to perish in the war and undoubtedly wouldn't be the last, but this hit close to home. He'd been courting a young lady from Charleston. In the last missive that he'd received from him, Marshall was informed of McDowell's intentions to ask that sweet girl for her hand in marriage.

Had they married before his untimely death? If so, there was one more Confederate widow to add to the ever-growing tally.

Chapter XXXIX

Alice had given her disguise quite a deal of thought. The advantage of pretending to be a Sisters of Mercy postulant was that wearing the wimple would completely cover her hair – a telltale sign of her heritage. However, religious sisters were not all that common in northern Georgia, so dressing as one may actually bring her more attention than less.

That being the case, she chose to go with the alternate plan. She would pass herself off as an upper-crust Caucasian female. When she'd worked in the big house as Susanna's handmaid, she'd learned the art of putting on airs. The chit had been an expert in the field.

A solid plan formulated in her mind. She'd dress up in widow's weeds. Wearing black head to foot – including a bonnet which would easily cover her hair – would make it simple enough to pass herself off as the wife of a young Confederate officer. With a dark veil to cover her face and matching black gloves, she'd be able to fool the most astute observer.

Marshall had told her of his classmate, Cadet Ranger McDowell, who was killed in action last year. She'd concoct a tale about how she and the young soldier had met when he was studying at The Citadel. They'd fallen madly in love, and before the Cadet Rangers were called up, they'd been married at the church downtown.

Alice could not imagine any reason that she'd be grilled further about her "husband." But, if anyone was more inquisitive, she'd just tell them that it pained her too much to speak of the inestimable man who'd given his life for the Confederacy.

With that figured out, she'd have to fabricate a valid reason for visiting the plantation.

Alice was wont to use the logical quadrant of her brain, but she could tap into her creative side if necessary. And now was just the time. A thought came to her. She'd arrive on the doorstep of Rosewood Plantation with the story that she was a young widow with a sizeable inheritance.

As her late husband had roots in Georgia, she was determined to settle down near his family's homestead. She'd stop by the plantation with the premise that she was in the market to buy slaves to run a place of her own... Perhaps see how their enterprise operated.

While on the property, she'd keep her eyes open for Gabrielle, Juliette and Jacques, and once she spotted them, she'd come up with a plan for whisking them away.

As fate would have it, the trunks that she, Marcus and Daisy had arrived in at the Sisters of Mercy convent had never been fully unpacked, so she had her share of clothes to rummage through for a costume. It turned out that Brigid had owned an entire black ensemble. She must have lost a loved one not so long ago.

With permission from the sisters to borrow the wagon with the concealed compartment for her trip, Alice had everything in place for her rescue mission.

"Remember, O most gracious Virgin Mary," she prayed quietly, "that never was it known that anyone who fled to thy protection, implored thy help or sought thine intercession was left unaided. Inspired with this confidence, I fly unto thee, O Virgin of virgins, my Mother; to thee do I come, before thee I stand, sinful and sorrowful. O Mother of the Word Incarnate, despise not my petitions, but in thy mercy hear and answer me. Amen."

Mother Mary, be a mother to me now.

Chapter XL

Marshall rode Maximus south from Cartersville. He'd been instructed to meet up with a group of soldiers in Marietta who were also traveling to South Carolina. There was safety in numbers. With each passing day, Sherman and his troops got closer to the northern border of Georgia, his eyes fixed on the prize of Atlanta.

More than likely, Union scouting parties were infiltrating the state already. A single Confederate soldier on horseback would be a sitting duck for a band of sharpshooting Yanks, so he'd be glad for the company.

His goal was to make it to Marietta by noon so he could hit the mess hall with the other soldiers before getting on the road again.

As he'd gotten a later start than he'd hoped, he set Maximus at a quick pace as they made their way down the main route from Cartersville to Marietta. Ten miles or so from his destination, he spotted a horse-drawn vehicle traveling in the same direction as he was. It appeared to be piloted by a woman.

Getting closer, there was no doubt that it was a female. One in mourning at that. Every last inch of her was bedecked in black.

Slowing his pace to keep from startling the horse pulling the wagon, Marshall perused the driver closer. The silhouette of the woman, with her shoulders pulled back and head held high, reminded him of someone he knew. And not in just a casual way.

It can't be, can it? He scrunched his eyes to refocus.

That reaffirmed what he saw. Just to be sure, he casually pulled Maximus alongside the vehicle and took a sideways glance at the profile of the young lady.

With her chin titled up like royalty, holding herself in a fashion that would give Cleopatra a run for her money, it was no wonder people considered her a princess.

Marshall began to think God had a peculiar sense of humor. Or, maybe He had a soft spot for lovestruck Confederate soldiers. Because one more time, against all odds, the Almighty Creator had deigned to let his life intersect with Alice's.

"Look what we've got here," said Marshall in a singsong voice. "My oh my."

Alice apparently wasn't ready to let go of her ruse. Tilting her chin higher, she replied in her most uppity voice. "I beg your pardon?"

If that curvaceous body hadn't given her away, the voice certainly would have. The slight French accent layered beneath the practiced Southern drawl was unmistakable.

"Fancy meeting you here."

The girl scowled and murmured something under her breath. He remembered enough French from school to know that it wasn't very ladylike.

"Well, Miss Alice, it seems as though we need to talk again. Mind pulling the wagon over for a spell?"

Letting out a sigh, she tugged the reins to bring the horse to a stop.

Marshall swung off Maximus and tethered him to the back of the wagon.

"Conveniently enough, there's trees just over there. How about we take a nice walk through the forest and we can chat about this joy ride you're taking today."

"To be honest," said Alice, "I'd rather not. I've a schedule to keep. I'm sure that you do as well."

"Never too busy to spend time with an exquisite young lady like yourself."

She eyed him skeptically. Whether she doubted that his schedule was that flexible or she questioned the sincerity of his compliment, he wasn't sure. Regardless, there was no way in heck that he'd let her go without finding out what was being calculated in that cunning mind of hers.

Looking as though they were setting off on a leisurely stroll, Marshall took Alice's elbow in his grasp and steered her toward the trees. Once in the seclusion of the forest, he commenced the inquest.

"Did you or did you not tell me that you would be traveling to Camp Nelson with Marcus, Daisy and the babies?"

"That was *your* interpretation of our conversation, Marshall." She put her hands on her hips and braced for the next question.

"You have me there. That was precisely how I'd interpreted that conversation. If I recall, you said something along the lines of a plan for the group to make its way to Kentucky."

"That's where the misunderstanding came in. I said the plans were for *the* group to travel to Kentucky. I never said that *I* was part of the group.

"I see."

"It's a matter of semantics."

"Of course. Well, now that we have that point cleared up, let's go on to the next one, shall we?"

Alice didn't appear to be all that keen on proceeding,

but there was no going back. He wasn't going to leave this spot until he got every last bit of information out of her.

"From what I gather, your plan from the get-go was to send the man whom you consider to be your brother with his woman and child north with the hopes of them being tucked away securely at Camp Nelson. You had no intention of accompanying them yourself, now did you?"

"No, sir."

"And what of your son?"

Even with the veil shielding her face, Marshall saw the lady bite her lip in consternation.

"Out with it, Alice. I want to know exactly what is going on in that pretty little head of yours."

Chapter XLI

"Why didn't you make the prudent choice and travel with the others to Kentucky?" Marshall inquired.

Shoulders slumped, she replied. "I needed to come back. Other lives are depending on me."

"Alice, you can't save the entire world."

"I realize that, but I can save some people." She looked at Marshall pleadingly.

"Don't tell me that you're going back to Pecan Hall to help other slaves escape. Even with Stewart gone, there is no way to sneak back onto that plantation." His words sprang forth with conviction.

"The widows' weeds won't help, either," he added. "They didn't stop me from recognizing you. And they won't stop the whites or the slaves at the plantation from recognizing you either. You'd be apprehended the minute you stepped foot on their land."

She hesitated just long enough for a sliver of hope to flicker across Marshall's face.

"I have no intention to go back to Pecan Hall. Ever."

"Thank God you've come to your senses."

"Actually, my destination is Rosewood Plantation. Outside of Marietta."

Marshall clamped his jaw together and spoke through clenched teeth. "Who on earth could be there that would make it worth risking your life to try and spirit them away? Your mother is gone, Marcus and his family are on their way to freedom. There can't possibly be anyone else of that much concern to you."

"There is."

Marshall paused, awaiting her answer.

"My brother and two sisters."

His eyes opened wide. "A brother and two sisters? How could it be that we've spoken at length multiple times, and you never mentioned them to me before now?"

"You never asked."

"Why would I have asked?" His face reddened in exasperation. "You talked extensively of Marcus. Since he was, in essence, your adopted brother, I came to the conclusion that you had no biological siblings."

"Which is — case in point — why one should never assume anything, Marshall," she replied matter-of-factly.

He seemed underwhelmed with her tutelage.

"Is there anything else that you haven't told me, Alice?"

More than you want to know, Marshall, let me assure you.

As witty as that sounded, she chose to go with the safe option.

"Perhaps. But things will be disclosed on an as-needed basis."

Marshall ran his hands through his hair and shook his head in vexation. "I'm sure they will, Alice. I'm sure they will."

Chapter XLII

"As altruistic as your motives may be, you are not traveling any further into enemy territory," said Marshall emphatically.

"Would you like to make a wager on that, soldier?" Alice crossed her arms over her chest. She looked as if she meant business.

"I can stop you. I've got the authority of the Confederate Army backing me up."

"That may be true, but I don't think you're going to lord that authority over me, are you, Marshall?"

The hesitation before he replied told her that what she'd expressed rang true.

"Maybe not... but I won't allow you to do this. At least not on your own. You're in over your head."

"For your information, I have every intention of doing this on my own. I'm their only surviving relative. They're my responsibility. No one else."

"Responsible for them? When was the last time you saw each other? They may not even remember they have an older sister."

That jab hit home. But it wouldn't deter her.

"Regardless, I mean to free them. Before first light tomorrow, they will be safely ensconced at the Sisters of Mercy convent in Cartersville. With Marcus and Daisy delivered safely, the sisters will simply retrace their path and bring Gabrielle, Juliette and Jacques to Camp Nelson as well."

"Then what will become of you?" Marshall asked pointedly.

"Seeing that there's a good chance that money is already placed on my head, I'll throw the dogs off their tracks and make my way west."

"West? That's a lot of territory you're talking about. Any specific plans?"

"Of course. There's always a plan." *For as many hours as we'd spent together, you'd think he'd know that about me by now.*

As he was watching her expectantly, she filled him in. "Miss Brigid is studying for the religious life in Little Rock. I intend to join her there."

"You're taking religious vows?" Marshall's voice rose in concern.

This man really was clueless.

"No. I'll be laying low there until the war concludes."

She couldn't help herself and had to egg him on a bit. "What concern would it be of yours if I had chosen to live the life of a religious sister?" she asked innocently.

"I would not be in favor of that."

"Why on earth not?"

"Well, for one thing, you have a child to take care of."

"Obviously, I wouldn't be a typical recruit, but I would imagine that things could be worked out if I was determined to travel that path."

"Well, I don't see you as a sister." Marshall sputtered. He glanced up as though he was picturing something in his head. "No, I see you as someone's wife. Some man's helpmeet. Married to a fellow who'd love you so much that he'd accept Josiah as his own and vow to make him a big brother someday."

Alice watched him in consternation. This was not how she'd imagined the conversation leading.

Her staring must have gotten to him. Marshall

suddenly appeared to be uncomfortable. "But that's neither here nor there at the moment. You need to tell me how you intend to free your brother and sisters."

"Why?"

"Because, once I've been given the step-by-step strategy that you've concocted to get on the plantation grounds without sounding the alarm, then I'll tell you how that plan can be enhanced with my help."

"Oh, really?" She raised her eyebrows.

As skeptical as she was, she laid out her plot, leaving no detail unaccounted for.

Marshall listened intently, nodding as she went along.

"That's well-laid out; I'll give you that."

Alice accepted the compliment in stride.

"Now, here's where I come in."

Her face fell. She didn't like the sound of that. The fewer people involved, the better. The last thing that she wanted was this man — for whom she harbored deep feelings of affection — to face a court-martial for assisting fugitive slaves.

"It's a sound plan," he continued. "However, tongues will be a waggin' if some strange woman shows up on the plantation doorstep, unaccompanied by a male, especially seeing that we're in the middle of a war."

He had a point. *Why hadn't I thought of that?*

"This is *my* proposal. "I'm sporting this fancy Confederate gear. May as well make good use of it. We'll tell the good folks at Rosewood Plantation that you're the widow of my old Citadel bunkmate McDowell and, out of respect for my deceased friend, I've agreed to escort you around the area in the hopes of securing some property to buy."

"Won't people wonder why you aren't doing soldier duty?" she asked warily.

"I can say I'm recuperating from internal injuries from some skirmish. There's always a scuffle going on somewhere or other in the area."

As much as she hated to admit it, his input really did enhance her plan.

"Heck," Marshall added. "If they still don't buy the story, I'll tell them I snuck from camp to spend some time with the girl that I've grown to love."

For once, Alice was speechless.

Chapter XLIII

With everything ironed out, the plan was set into motion. On the one hand, having Marshall accompany her gave Alice a sense of security. On the other hand, she felt slightly unsettled with him around. She detested the thought of putting his safety in jeopardy.

They pulled up to Rosewood Plantation in the early afternoon. A stable hand took the reins from Alice to secure the horse to the hitching post. Marshall sprung from the carriage and helped her down, his hands staying on her waist a moment longer than necessary. She certainly didn't mind but didn't want to raise any eyebrows, so she inched away from him, nodding her head in thanks.

With the soldier directly on her heels, she strode up the front walk, adjusted the black veil covering her face, went up the porch steps and gave a solid tug on the string for the doorbell. A Negro man, dressed in butler attire, answered her summons. The questioning look that he gave Alice caused her some alarm. *Maybe this costume isn't as good as I thought it was.*

Seeing as there was nothing that could be done at the moment anyhow, she plowed ahead. When Alice informed the man that she was there to speak with the owner of the plantation, he ushered her and Marshall into the foyer and excused himself to summon his master.

A few minutes later, a finely appointed elderly man stepped into the foyer. Alice did her best to hide her surprise. It had been a few years since she saw Mr. Williams' brother-in-law, but unless the man had oddly been aged by the ravages of war, this was not him. Were they at the wrong plantation?

"May I help you?" he inquired.

"I hope so, sir. I stopped by today to see Mr. Smythe. This is his house, is it not?"

"It was," the man replied. "But I bought the place from him and his wife just before the war broke out."

"Oh, really? I hadn't heard that they'd moved." Alice did her best to hide the disappointment from her voice. "Do you have any idea as to where the family has relocated?"

"From what I recall, they had plans to move back East. The gentleman hailed from a coastal state."

"East? So, they're not running a plantation any longer?"

"Not as far as I know."

"Then you took possession of their stock? Human and animal?" She clenched her fists, praying that the answer would be yes.

"No, ma'am. They sold all their possessions before they left."

Alice ground her teeth in frustration.

"Oh, I see. Someone got a fine deal, I would think. The quality of their slaves was second to none. I'd had my eye on a couple of them. Did one of the gentlemen on a neighboring plantation buy them by chance?"

"Weren't purchased by a man. It was a woman."

"A lady?" Alice put her hand over her heart in shock. It wasn't feigned by any means. "How unconventional. Would you happen to know who this lady was?"

"I certainly do. It was Elizabeth Felten. Wife of Dr. Willis Felten. After they got married, she relocated from DeKalb County to his plantation."

The possibility of tracking down her siblings was getting more remote by the minute.

"Well, that would certainly make sense. And that plantation is...?"

"Somewhere up near Cartersville."

Alice's eyes widened. *Did I hear him correctly?*

"Cartersville? That's a lovely area," she gave the man a smile. "Well, we don't want to use up any more of your time. You take care of yourself."

"You too, ma'am. Sorry for your loss."

It took a moment for his comment to register. She'd forgotten about the widow ruse.

"You're so kind." Alice gushed, nodding her head in thanks. She took her leave with Marshall in her shadow.

Once they were back on the bench seat of the wagon, the soldier shook his head in admiration.

"You ever think of taking up law, Miss Alice? That was quite the line of questioning."

"If I had the means to set up a practice, I would certainly consider it."

"We'll have to see if we can make that happen."

Alice peered at him curiously. The way he pronounced that statement, a person might believe that such a thing was possible. A woman practicing law would be an achievement in and of itself. A colored woman practicing law? That would be ground-breaking, to say the least.

"I may regret asking this, but what's your plan from here, Alice?"

"Heading back to Cartersville, of course."

Marshall let out a deep sigh as if dealing with a petulant child. "Of course."

"You certainly don't have to accompany me."

"Like heck, I don't. Who knows what trouble you'll get into next?"

"Trouble? It's quite the opposite. I'm helping get people *out* of trouble."

"That's one way to look at it, Alice."

Chapter XLIV

Marshall ran through a list of excuses that he could offer his commanding officer for reporting to Marietta a week late. Aiding and abetting a fugitive would be the honest reason, but he didn't know if that disclosure would sit too well with the man.

He had no complaints about spending another full day alongside Alice. Heck, he'd probably consider going AWOL just for that opportunity alone.

As for the discussion with the upper brass, he'd cross that bridge when he came to it. In the meantime, he meant to enjoy every last minute with this remarkable girl. It was impossible to foretell if they'd ever meet again.

As they pulled away from Rosewood Plantation, Marshall pondered how to start the conversation. Was now the time to confess to Alice how he really felt about her? Should they chit-chat for a while to get the words flowing? He could start by asking about her life and growing up years, since apparently, she hadn't been too forthcoming up until now.

What the heck. He'd never been one to pussyfoot around a topic. He'd get the biggest thing off his chest first and circle back to the small talk later.

"Alice?" He waited until her eyes were on his and then proceeded. "Remember how I joked that I'd tell the plantation owner that I'd snuck from camp to spend some time with the girl that I'd grown to love?"

"Yes," she replied tentatively.

"I wasn't kidding. Well, technically, the 'snuck from camp' part would have been fabricated, but the other words came straight from my heart."

He paused, feeling a bit awkward, a sensation that was generally foreign to him. But he wanted his words to come out right.

Turning his head back to keep his eyes on the road, he blurted out. "I have actually grown to love you, Alice."

His eyes shifted her way. Cool as a cucumber. *She's good.*

"Anything you want to say to me, miss?"

She hesitated, as if considering her words. Finally, she spoke up.

"So, what was life like for you as a youngster, Marshall?"

Guess we're going with the small talk. It was better than nothing, though.

"Just your average childhood, I'd say."

She stared at him as if expecting more, so he continued. "It was just me and mama and my father. They were married a long time before I came around. I was a late-in-life blessing for them."

"I'm sure you were," she noted with humor in her voice.

"At least, that's what mama tells me," he said with a chuckle. "I grew up in the heart of Charleston. My father ran an import business. Went to a public school for elementary and secondary education. Got accepted at The Citadel, class of 1862."

"I'll bet you were a mama's boy," she teased.

"You could say that. However, my father did not allow me to be coddled. He was in charge of my discipline."

"I can't imagine you were that unruly."

"Unruly, no. Mischievous, absolutely. I got in my share of trouble. Lucky for me, I developed a talent for talking my way out of it."

"Can't say I'm surprised to hear that. Law truly must be your calling."

"I'd say it is."

"What about the young ladies? I'm sure you charmed your share in the day."

"Guilty as charged. But it was all in fun. A few of them set their sights on me, but none of them ever really caught my fancy. At least not for more than a week or two."

"A heartbreaker then. I can see that," said Alice jokingly.

"I wouldn't say that. I never said anything to lead them to believe I was looking for a long-term commitment."

"Why ever not? I'm sure Charleston has its share of beauties."

"You're right about that. But, as hard as this may be for you to believe, I was searching for more than just a pretty face. I wanted someone who'd challenge me. Smart, witty, express opinions of her own — not just parroting her father's thoughts."

His eyes shifted up to the right as he continued. "For mama's sake, I was hoping to find a good Catholic girl. For my sake, it wouldn't hurt if she was pretty."

"Are you going to tell me, Marshall, that in all your years of interacting with members of the opposite sex, you never found a girl who met all your requirements?"

"Oh, I did all right."

"So, what has become of this wonderous female?"
"She's sitting right next to me."

Chapter XLV

Alice forced her jaw shut. For the life of her, she couldn't understand what made Marshall tick. He acted as though he were courting her. What were his intentions?

She intended to find out before they went any further. There was no use continuing this charade, as they both knew that it would lead nowhere.

"Marshall, we need to be honest with each other."

"I was under the impression that we have been," he said guardedly.

The way his eyes bored into hers, she was losing her train of thought. Shaking her head to come back to her senses, she continued.

"Perhaps I should have worded that differently. I need to be honest with myself."

He knit his brows together and waited for her to continue.

"When I listen to your sentiments, I almost forget my circumstances and think that we could actually create a life together." She pursed her lips as she sought her next words.

"Marshall, where is this going? You shower me with words of endearment, but I don't see how we can further this relationship."

He opened his mouth to respond, but she placed her finger over his lips to silence him.

"As enjoyable as it would be to dream, you and I can never have a future together."

"That's not true."

"It *is* true, Marshall. Almost every state in the Union has laws forbidding interracial marriages. Just last year, the term miscegenation — interbreeding of people of different races — was coined. Journalists meant to stir up fear over such a thing becoming widespread should slavery as a whole be abolished."

He looked at her skeptically. "And, so what?"

"Mixed couples could be charged with adultery should they be caught applying for a marriage license."

"What would you say if I told you that I didn't give a rat's A-S-S what the laws say," Marshall stated forcibly.

That wasn't the answer that she'd expected. She had no retort on the tip of her tongue.

"You want to live your life without people sticking their noses in your business?" he questioned. "Then you got to get away to God's country. A state so vast you may never see your neighbors if you don't have a mind to."

Alice cocked her head questioningly.

"I'm talking about Texas."

Is he saying what I think he's saying?

"A man and woman could have a life there and live as they please. No one would be any the wiser."

"Where are you going with this conversation, Marshall?"

"I'm saying that two people like you and me could create a life for ourselves in that wide-open land."

Not knowing how to adequately respond to his statement, she changed the subject.

"It won't be long before we get back to Cartersville. Should be easy enough to find the Felten plantation," she noted. "Shall we recreate the ruse that I'm a young widow of means, with the intent to buy property and slaves to start my own enterprise?"

Marshall gave her a smirk. She wasn't off the hook.

Nonetheless, he answered her question. "That sounds prudent to me. Shall we practice our lines? You can play the role of the grieving Mrs. McDowell, and I'll play the role of Elizabeth Felten."

Clearing his throat, Marshall began to speak in a falsetto voice, which, despite the gravity of the situation, caused Alice to laugh.

They rehearsed their lines for the rest of the trip. When they got to Cartersville, it took just one stop to find a person who could direct them to the Felten plantation.

Following the same enactment performed at the other plantation, they fell right into their roles when Mrs. Felten greeted them at the front door.

"Mrs. Felten, it's such a pleasure to meet you," said Alice amiably. "My name is Mrs. McDowell. My late husband was Lieutenant G.M. McDowell." She paused for effect. "He was killed in action at Gettysburg."

"You have my condolences, ma'am," the woman replied sincerely.

"Thank you." Alice dabbed her eyelashes with a lacey handkerchief.

"First Lieutenant Kent," she said, indicating Marshall, "was my husband's bunkmate at The Citadel. He's been kind enough to accompany me today."

"It's a pleasure to meet you both," said the woman. "How may I be of service to you?"

Alice went into her rehearsed spiel about being widowed, left with an inheritance enough to purchase her own plantation, and being in the market for slaves.

"As you can imagine, with so many Negroes taking

flight during the turbulence of the war, it's not easy finding help," said Alice.

"I completely understand," said Mrs. Felten. "But, tell me, what has that to do with me?"

"Seeing that your plantation is the largest one in Cartersville, I thought perhaps you might have a slave or two you'd be willing to part with. If the price was right, of course."

"I'd love to help you, Mrs. McDowell, but I've had a hard enough time keeping my staff as it is. Those abolitionists think nothing of being party to theft and helping slaves take flight to the free states."

"The nerve!" Alice exclaimed.

"I understand that stock is limited now, Mrs. Felten, but I'm in a fix. I'd be willing to pay you one hundred dollars. Greenbacks."

A startled look came across the woman's face before she composed herself again. "One hundred dollars? For how many slaves?"

"That would be one-hundred dollars apiece."

"Apiece? Greenbacks, did you say?"

"Yes, that's correct."

The woman's eyes lit up in greed. "Would that be house slaves or field hands?"

"That's to be determined. I'd like to see the house selection first."

"Of course." The woman clapped her hands to beckon a maid.

"Missy, gather up all the household help in the parlor immediately."

"Yes'm," the black woman replied.

In less than five minutes, eight people lined the far wall of the parlor. Immediately, Alice spotted her siblings. Yet, she deliberately made a show of leisurely walking down the line and inspecting each person.

It didn't appear that Juliette and Jacques recognized her. But the way Gabrielle's eyes widened when Alice approached assured her that the girl knew who she was.

She grasped Gabrielle's hand to pull her closer and slipped a tiny bit of paper into her palm. That done, she had the girl pirouette as if being inspected from all sides.

After making a show of scrutinizing the rest of the servants, she turned to Mrs. Felten.

"It does make sense to stock the house help first. If you'd be so kind to give me a day to think this over, I'll stop back late tomorrow and let you know which of the Negroes I'm interested in purchasing."

"Fair enough," replied the older lady.

"Thank you again for your time, Mrs. Felten. You have a fine selection of slaves here. It will take some deliberating to come to a decision."

The slaves were dismissed, and she and Marshall made their goodbyes to their hostess.

Back in the carriage, Alice could hardly contain her joy.

"Was that your sister, then?" Marshall asked.

"Not just one sister but both sisters and my younger brother."

She turned and gave Marshall a full smile. "I've hit paydirt!"

"I wouldn't count your chickens before they're hatched, Alice. We still need to get them off the property."

"It's just a matter of meeting them at the chosen spot

tonight. I slipped a message into Gabrielle's palm. It was written *en francais*, so even if it would be spotted by someone, I doubt if they'd be able to translate it."

Alice couldn't contain herself and clapped her hands together in glee.

"If we can pull this off, it almost makes me think we can pull anything off."

She winked before turning to face the road again. Even using only her peripheral vision, she saw Marshall grinning ear to ear.

Chapter XLVI

How hadn't I noticed those dimples before? Maybe because Alice hadn't had reason to smile so widely up until this point. *If I have my say, I'll keep her smiling like that for the rest of her life.*

Then his own face lit up. Did he interpret her words correctly? If so, that means that she, too, believed that they could have a life together. A Bible verse flashed in his mind's eye. "I can do all things through Christ who strengthens me." The thought gave him hope. He whistled all the way back into town.

The two of them made their way to the general store. They needed provisions for the fugitives. He didn't want to send them to the Sisters of Mercy empty-handed.

"You can just go in," said Alice. "I'll wait out here."

"Oh, no, little lady. I understand your discomfort mingling amongst the townsfolk, but you need to do this. Assert yourself as a privileged landowner. If you want to pull this whole charade off, you need to keep practicing. This is as good a place as any."

Looking up to the left as though calculating the risk, she acquiesced and allowed Marshall to help her alight from the wagon. Pulling her shoulders back, she slipped her hand into the crook of his arm and walked with him into the building.

Once inside, the two of them browsed side by side, choosing enough dried and canned goods to get the youngsters through until they reached Camp Nelson.

Even though he assured Alice that he had more than enough money to cover the purchases, she chose just the essentials, which in his mind didn't seem enough for three people taking that long of a trip. He couldn't convince her to buy more.

Marshall excused himself to inspect the horse gear. While he did that, he noticed Alice peering into the glass-enclosed front case. The store owner noticed as well and solicitously offered to bring out some merchandise for her to inspect closer.

Feeling her glancing his way, Marshall pretended to be engrossed in a tack and saddle display. When she turned back to the counter, he surreptitiously glanced over to see what had caught her eye.

The proprietor had produced a square of velvet with several pieces of jewelry laid upon it. When the gentleman stepped away to finish another task, allowing her time to shop, he saw Alice slip the glove off her left hand. She slid a ring onto her finger. Holding her hand straight forward, she admired the smooth gold band with a ruby set square in the middle of it. As she turned her hand to and fro, the ruby caught the sun's rays, and the reflection reached to the wall nearest him.

From what he could tell, the ring was the perfect fit. Giving it one last appraisal, Alice reluctantly slid it off her finger and laid it back onto the velvet.

After stalling a few seconds, Marshall cleared his throat to catch Alice's attention and then made his way back to the counter. That gave her enough time to push the fabric into the hands of the store owner and swing around.

"Ready, ma'am?"

"I... I am, thank you." She took one last glance at the display case behind her.

"I'll walk you to the vehicle and then carry our purchases out. Shall we?" He extended his arm to her. As before, she put her hand into the crook of his elbow. She then turned to thank the man who'd been helping her.

After Alice was settled on the wagon seat, Marshall walked back into the store. As the shopkeeper tallied his bill, he peered through the glass and eyed the ruby ring nestled on the velvet.

"That'll be one dollar and twenty-eight cents," said the proprietor, pushing the stub of a pencil behind his ear.

"I'd like to add one more item to the tally, if I may."

"Of course," the man replied, pulling the pencil out again.

"I'll take that ring too," said Marshall, pointing to the ruby ring.

The man's eyes opened wide in astonishment. "That ring'll set you back twenty-five dollars."

"That it will, but worth every penny, let me assure you."

Cheerily, the clerk pulled the ring from its spot, wrapped it in a piece of silk and tucked it into a small velvet bag. He pulled the drawstring tight to secure the piece of jewelry inside and then handed it to Marshall. "Here you go, First Lieutenant."

Marshall tucked the bag into the breast pocket of his jacket.

"That's one lucky lady you have there, young man."

"To tell you the truth, I'm the lucky one," he replied happily.

Nodding to the man, Marshall grabbed the rest of the merchandise and stepped out of the building. With Alice watching, he secured everything in the back of the wagon, took his seat and cracked the whip over the horse's head.

For a while, the two of them drove in silence. Marshall couldn't stop thinking about the ring and what his next step would be. The joy he felt sitting next to that young lady caused his heart to beat so wildly that he wondered if she could hear it from her seat.

Alice was one to guard her feelings, so it was hard to say exactly what she felt, but if she cared about him even one-tenth as much as he cared about her, things would be going his way.

As a younger man, Marshall had experienced moments of puppy love, but those instances were nothing compared to what he was now feeling. Alice had every attribute he'd want in a wife and then some. He couldn't get over his good fortune and the blessed turn of events in his life.

The two of them drove to the edge of town to bide their time until nightfall. Marshall was ecstatic to spend more time in Alice's company. He planned to store each moment in his memory bank. Although he had the ring and he fully intended to present it to her soon, this was not the time nor the place. He fervently hoped that God intended for them to be together at some point, but nothing was sure at this moment. Where their lives would go over the next few months was anyone's guess.

Finding a secluded spot, he unhitched the horse from the vehicle and tied it to a tree so it could graze while they waited. After he helped Alice disembark, he grabbed a blanket from the back of the wagon and spread it on the ground to create space for a picnic lunch. They had fresh fruit and some bread they'd just purchased.

The two of them spent the rest of the day talking. Marshall had never met a female before with whom he could so easily engage in conversation. Alice listened carefully as he detailed his past, his time in the military and his plans for the future.

While she wasn't as forthcoming about her life as he was, she wasn't averse to answering a direct question. Although he'd been surrounded by people of color his whole life, he'd never actually spoken in such depth to anyone of a different ethnicity than his own before.

Her description of life in bondage was eye-opening. Everything from the harrowing tales of the atrocities committed by slaveowners to the bits of joviality that the blacks were able to find in their mundane and difficult lives.

Even though Alice had what she called the "fortune" of being a house slave and not subjected to the rigorous labor in the fields and scrutiny by the overseers, she still had a difficult existence, one to which no human being should ever be subjected. His mind wandered back to Stewart and what he'd put her through. Anger toward that reprobate coursed through his veins.

Well into their tete-a-tete, Marshall instinctively pulled Alice's hands into his. She stiffened at first, and a blush came to her cheeks, but in time she relaxed and returned his grip. With the sun teetering on the edge of the horizon, he knew that they needed to wrap up their conversation.

As strange as it sounded, seeing that the country was

in the midst of a civil war, this was one of the best days of his life. For a few hours, he'd been able to put everything behind him and dream of a future. A future, God willing, with this young woman whom he loved more and more with each passing minute.

Their words died down. Reluctantly he stood up, tugging on Alice's hands to bring her to her feet as well. He wrapped her in his arms, and they stood molded together, watching the final rays of light fade from the sky.

Trying not to let his disappointment show, Marshall pulled back and gently cupped Alice's face in his hands. Sensing no skittishness in her, he bent down and brushed his lips against hers.

As she seemed amenable to that, he decided to give her a real kiss, hoping it was the first of a million that they'd share in their life together.

Just as he leaned towards her, the horse whinnied as though something had startled it. With that, the spell was broken. Marshall pulled back but vowed to himself to resume where he'd left off when they were together again. He just prayed it'd be on this side of the earthly plane.

Chapter XLVII

A sigh escaped Alice's lips. That was inopportune timing. It was probably just as well anyhow. No use sealing a promise with a kiss if a promise hadn't actually been voiced.

She and Marshall scoured the woods, looking to determine what had startled the horse. But, the only movements that they noticed were squirrels scurrying here and there and a few birds flitting in the treetops.

The sun made its final descent behind the horizon, and darkness shrouded the wooded area in which they were ensconced. Alice had written "*dix chaussée*" on the slip of paper that she'd handed to Gabrielle. She prayed that the younger girl had interpreted the message correctly and would bring Juliette and Jacques to meet her and Marshall on the road that ran alongside the Felten property at ten o'clock.

It may have been a stretch providing Gabrielle with such a cryptic message, but Alice had to be cautious in case the paper was discovered. Hopefully, her siblings would be in the designated area at the assigned time.

Making the Sign of the Cross, she grabbed Marshall's extended hand as he walked the horse and wagon out of the woods and onto the road. Thanks to the clouds overhead, they were completely engulfed in darkness as they embarked on their trip to the plantation.

"Let's go over the plan one more time, Marshall."

"Yes, ma'am," he replied sardonically. *Apparently, he thinks a half-dozen times is enough. Maybe for some people, but not for me.*

Alice ticked off the instructions on her fingers one by one. "We drive by the plantation. Once we're past the property line, I'll make my way back to the edge of their land, crouch down and follow the hedge line to avoid detection from anyone in the main house. In the meantime, if you see anyone coming — either from the road or the house — you'll reproduce the call of a mourning dove."

She glanced toward Marshall expectantly. Dutifully, he gave his best impression of the aforementioned bird. Alice couldn't help but wince.

"It'll have to do."

Marshall chuckled and then gave her his full attention again as she continued.

"Once I've found the children, we'll make our way back along the hedge line to the wagon. I'll have them climb into the compartment under the floorboards. After that, it's just a matter of getting them to the convent."

"And, if we're noticed?"

"If someone on the planation raises the alarm, we put the horse to the test and race off. We'll have a head start, and none of their mounts will be saddled, so that should give us a ten-minute lead, more than enough to make it ahead of them to the safety of the church."

"What if we're approached by someone on horse, either coming toward us or from behind?"

"If we're questioned, we'll go with the story that I've been widowed, and you're fulfilling a promise to your deceased bunkmate that you would make sure that I'm taken care of. You're bringing me back to my family home."

Alice ran through everything in her head one more time before resuming the discussion. "Is there anything I've missed?"

"Just one minor detail," Marshall said, a grin coming to his face.

She glanced at him quizzically.

"What if you're asked for proof of marriage?"

"Do you think anyone would actually do that?" Her brow furrowed.

"You never know."

"Hmm."

"It's all right. I've got that covered."

At that very moment, the clouds skittered away, and beams from the moon lit up the area surrounding them. Marshall pulled the wagon to a halt and reached into the breast pocket of his overcoat and produced a small bag, which he handed to her.

Her heart pounding, Alice untied the string and emptied the pouch into her hand. Unwrapping a piece of velvet, she couldn't believe her eyes. It was the ring that she'd been admiring in the general store that afternoon.

She tilted her head up to look Marshall straight in the eyes. Her mouth opened, but no words came out.

"Try it on," he prodded.

Mechanically, she slid the ring onto her left ring finger. It fit just as perfectly as it had several hours before. She didn't know what to say.

"Alice, I want you to have this ring as a promise. Promise that you'll wait for me. If you and I make it unscathed through this war, we'll find each other."

"Find each other? And then what?"

"And then I'll court you properly and, when the time

is right, I'll drop to one knee and formally ask for your hand in marriage."

"Marriage?" Her jaw dropped in astonishment. "Are you sure? We barely know each other."

"I knew from the moment that I laid eyes on you that you were the woman for me," Marshall admitted sincerely.

"You did?" Alice asked in astonishment. A thought came to her. "What of Josiah?"

"I'll raise him as my own son."

A broad smile came to Alice's face, her pearly teeth glinting in the moonlight.

"So, will you accept this ring?"

Alice nodded her head vigorously and threw her arms around Marshall.

Her voice caught in her throat. "I never dreamed that my life could possibly turn out so beautifully, Marshall. I will pray unceasingly for this war to end and for us to be back together soon."

"From your lips to God's ears," he replied with a laugh.

As much as Alice wanted to remain stopped alongside the road so she could revel in the moment and admire her ring closer, she knew that they needed to continue forward to make it to the plantation on time. Reluctantly, she took the ring off and put it back into the bag, slipping it into the pocket of her dress for safekeeping.

While Marshall kept his left hand on the reins, Alice wrapped his other hand between hers and snuggled up to his shoulder for the remainder of the trip. When the Felten plantation came into sight, she snapped back to her normal strict posture.

Giving her fingers one last squeeze, Marshall sat up ramrod straight himself.

"It's go time."

The wagon rolled past the estate, and once out of view of the house, he pulled over, and Alice bounded to the dirt road, not waiting for assistance. She was anxious to find her siblings.

Crouching down, she noiselessly made her way past the hedges. About a quarter of the way along, she heard someone whisper.

"Alais?"

She almost collapsed in relief. She'd know that voice anywhere. It was Gabrielle.

Chapter XLVIII

Marshall twisted in his seat, straining to keep his eyes on Alice. While he'd prefer to be the one skulking through the grass, he understood that this was something that she needed to do to reassure her brother and sisters that they were in safe hands.

He pulled his pocket watch from his overcoat. Two more minutes, and he was going after her. His patience was growing thin.

Finally, he saw movement in the grass, and four bodies appeared before him. Jumping down from the vehicle, he lifted the wagon's trap door to allow the children to crawl into the hidden space. That done, he assisted Alice to her spot on the bench and climbed back up to his seat.

With a slight tap of the reins to the horse's rump, they lurched forward. While his first thought had been to set the horse off at a canter, being as quiet as possible was critical at this moment, so he tamped down his impatience and settled into an unhurried pace.

After they were a half-mile or so from the plantation, he had the horse pick up its speed.

"I'll keep an eye out in front of us, you keep your eyes to the rear to see if anyone comes up from behind," he instructed Alice.

She turned in her seat, eyes glued to the road behind them. When they were within a mile of town, Marshall felt like he could finally let his breath out. He rolled his shoulders to loosen the knots that had been working their way up his back since they'd left the copse of trees.

No sooner had he done that when he felt Alice stiffen up next to him.

"Someone's coming," she whispered, fear in her voice.

Marshall whipped his head around. It was a lone rider. From the quick glance he had, he knew immediately that the man was a soldier. If it had been just another rider going about his business, he would have kept the horse going at the same speed so as to not arouse any suspicion.

But someone of the military persuasion presented a whole different set of considerations. If it was a Confederate soldier, Marshall would be busted for being AWOL. Conversely, if it was a Union soldier, he'd be captured, the vehicle would be searched, and the jig would be up.

He tried to come up with a quick solution, but before anything came to mind, Alice spoke.

"I've got it," she pronounced. "This may sound farfetched, but you're going to have to trust me."

His eyes were glued to hers, and he nodded in agreement.

"When I give you the word, I want you to push me off of the seat so that I tumble to the ground."

"Are you joking? I would never do that!"

"You must. Assuming the man is an honorable one, when he sees me in distress, he'll come to my aid rather than chase after you. Once I'm on the ground, I want you to race to the convent. The sisters will hide the wagon and take care of the children."

"I don't like this plan, Alice. There must be a better way."

"There may be, but at the moment, this is the best that I can come up with. No need to worry about me. I'll think of something to delay the man to give you enough time to make your escape."

Alice pried open Marshall's right hand, placed the small bag into it, and curled his fingers around it. Before he could react, she yelled, "Now!"

Instinctively, Marshall did as he was instructed and gave her a shove, albeit a gentle one, propelling her from the vehicle. Once he witnessed her hit the ground and roll several times toward the edge of the road, he cracked the whip over the horse's head and sped off.

It killed him seeing her sprawled out on the ground behind him, but he had to trust her good judgment and keep up his end of the deal so that the children would be safely delivered to the sisters. Lord knows what they were thinking in the back of the wagon as the horse raced into town.

When a cluster of buildings appeared on the horizon, Marshall slowed the horse down and approached the town limits at a brisk pace, yet one that wouldn't cause undue alarm. He patiently bade his time as they made their way to the convent.

Arriving at the property, he pulled the vehicle behind the main building to conceal it until it could be stashed in one of the outer buildings.

Springing from the seat, he spoke in a low voice to the children.

"We're here. I'm going to go wake the sisters so we can get you safely ensconced inside. Don't move until I get back."

No response meant that they were obeying, so he strode to the back of the convent and rapped soundly on the doorframe. Some thirty seconds later, an older woman, wearing a robe, appeared at the door.

"May I help you?" she asked warily.

"I'm delivering a package from Miss Alice."

Immediately the door swung wide open. "Of course, thank you, sir. Please come in."

"No disrespect, ma'am, but we've no time to waste. We were spotted on the trip over."

The woman nodded and stepped through the doorway in the direction that Marshall indicated. Once she got to the vehicle, she opened the trap door to reveal the three children huddled together, their eyes wide in fright.

"No need to be fearful children, you're safe here. Let's get you out of the wagon and into the convent."

One at a time, the children descended from the vehicle. After they were all on ground level, the sister escorted them into the residence. She then pointed in the direction of the barn and indicated that Marshall should park the conveyance there.

Before he set off to do that, he stepped back to the woman and gave her a brief summary of the situation. That done, he took care of the vehicle and then turned in the direction from whence he'd just come.

He sprinted off of the church property, praying in cadence to his steps. First and foremost, he prayed that Alice hadn't been injured during her hasty descent from the wagon. Second, he prayed that the man who found her was a gentleman and was treating her kindly. Lastly, he prayed that the soldier would bring Alice into Cartersville rather than back to Dallas. If it were the latter, he might never find her again.

Chapter XLIX

The sound of galloping hooves came to Alice's ears. Apparently, the soldier had witnessed her fall from the vehicle, as he'd set his horse off at a breakneck pace to reach her.

She kept her face to the ground and eyes closed as the man dismounted, stepped toward her and then dropped to his knees.

If this man is a Union soldier, this will make concocting a believable story considerably easier. She held her breath as the man put his hands underneath her to gently turn her to face him.

Doing her best to put on a plausible theatrical performance, she kept her eyes shut as the man addressed her.

"Miss," he croaked out, "are you all right?"

Dramatically, Alice fluttered her long eyelashes before opening her eyes. One peek at the man, and her heart fell to her stomach. A Confederate. And a young one at that. He couldn't have been any more than her age. *Drat!* So much for Plan A.

Time to set Plan B into motion. "Who... who are you?" she said weakly. "What happened to me?"

The man looked directly into her eyes. Alice was grateful to have the veil covering her face. Between that and the darkness of the night with the clouds overhead once again, her heritage should be concealed.

"Private Mason Burns, at your service."

Alice made as though she were attempting to get herself to a seated position. Seeing her struggle, the soldier put his arm around her to assist the process.

"Are you sure you can sit up, miss? That was a nasty spill you took. You may have broken something."

"A spill?" She shook her head slightly. Thank goodness she'd had the foresight to tuck and roll when she exited the conveyance, or his words would be true to life.

"Someone pushed you off a wagon," he exclaimed.

"What?" she put on a mask of confusion. "Why would anyone ever want to do such a thing as that?"

"I don't know, miss. Don't you remember?" The soldier's tone showed his concern. "You were riding alongside some gentleman. Or man, I should say. Any brute who'd push a woman off a moving vehicle would not be considered a gentleman in my eyes."

Hook, line and sinker. This pup is making this too easy.

Biting her lower lip, Alice replied. "I can't seem to think straight at this moment. Guess I must have taken a blow to the head if I really did fall from the wagon as you've said."

"Miss, I need to get you into town for some medical attention. I'm just coming from Dallas. I can take you back there, and we'll see the doc."

Going back to Dallas was the last thing that she wanted to do. There could be a posse heading from there searching for her at this very moment.

Calculating as quickly as she could, Alice came up with another option.

"Which way was the wagon that I was on traveling?"

"That way, miss," said the man pointing to the west.

"I'm assuming I was headed that way for a reason. Is there a town close by?"

"There is a town just a mile or so away, but it's so small, the only one practicing medicine there is the camp surgeon."

As much as she didn't want to go anywhere near a Confederate camp, Alice knew that Marshall and the children were in Cartersville. If she hoped to have any chance of him finding her, that was the logical place to travel.

"I'm sure a camp surgeon is just as good as any surgeon," she said, a slight smile coming to her face. "Besides, I may not even need to see a doctor. Other than a few bumps and bruises, I should be fine in two shakes of a lamb's tail."

"We'll see," the private answered, a reserved note in his voice.

"Thank you, sir. I'm so grateful that you came upon me. I can't imagine what I would have done if you hadn't come to my rescue." She batted her eyelashes at him.

As dark as it was, Alice was convinced that she saw his face go crimson.

"It was my pleasure, miss."

"Would you be able to assist me in getting off the ground?" she asked sweetly.

"Absolutely."

Gingerly the soldier scooped Alice up, one hand under her knees and the other supporting her back.

After a few moments of awkwardness, she asked him to set her on her feet so that she could get her bearings.

"Are you feeling steady enough for me to help you onto my horse?" Private Burns asked.

"I believe I am."

Once she was seated, the soldier hoisted himself up

behind her and then gave the horse the signal to walk.

The pace was painfully slow — seeing as her back was plastered to the soldier's chest — but they could have been traveling at a snail's pace, and it wouldn't have bothered her. The longer it took to get into town, the more time Marshall had to get the children under the sisters' wings.

Unfortunately, the town loomed before them in less time than she'd anticipated. Once they made their way through the first couple blocks, the private steered his horse to the south and proceeded to a neighborhood at the edge of town dotted with dozens of tents.

The thought of flinging herself off the horse and making a run for it crossed Alice's mind, but she doubted she'd get too far. She wasn't that familiar with the lay of the land to make it too far.

As they approached a full-sized tent, she tried to come up with some reason to avoid meeting the doctor. She gave the soldier her best justifications for skipping an examination, but he wouldn't be swayed.

With no way out of the situation, Alice let the man help her dismount and escort her into the medical tent.

The surgeon was tending an injured soldier, but when he stepped away from the cot, Burns got his attention and described the scenario that he'd happened upon.

Eying Alice up and down, the man wearily responded. "From what I can see, she seems to be fine."

"That's exactly what I told Private Burns," exclaimed Alice. "I don't want to waste your time, sir." A sliver of hope came to her. The sooner she got out of the medical tent, the sooner she could make her way off the encampment grounds.

"No problem, miss. As long as you're here, we may as well take a look at you. Please lay down on this cot."

Burns excused himself and stepped outside the tent.

"Let me assure you, sir, I'm perfectly fine," said Alice hastily.

That confounded man wouldn't take no for an answer either. Begrudgingly, she complied and laid on the cot. She closed her eyes as the man probed her skull with her fingertips, checking for bumps or contusions.

"Let's get this out of the way, shall we?" he suggested.

Alice screwed her eyes shut tightly. She felt a slight breeze as the veil was lifted from her face.

There was a moment's pause, then the surgeon barked out, "Private, you need to get back in here and see something."

Chapter L

Luckily, Marshall had managed to step behind a large oak tree just as a horse with a male and female atop it plodded past him on the main road leading into town.

He was relieved to see Alice seated on the front portion of the saddle. Now it was just a matter of discreetly following the pair to determine their destination.

Seeing that the man who'd picked her up was a soldier, Marshall guessed that they were heading toward an encampment. After a few minutes of trailing them, he found that his deduction was accurate.

Wearing a Confederate uniform, it shouldn't cause too much of a stir if he slipped into the camp. He jammed his slouch hat low over his forehead and followed the horse from a few yards back as it stepped its way around the numerous tents pitched on the grounds.

A large box tent indicated either the officer quarters or the surgical tent. Marshall prayed that it was the latter. Otherwise, that would indicate that Alice's subterfuge had already been discovered.

With the tent flap pulled back, he verified that it was indeed the field surgeon's headquarters. He stepped behind the tent to listen in on the conversation between the private and the doctor.

All seemed to go well until the younger man walked out, leaving the physician alone with Alice. Less than thirty seconds later, the man called the private back into the tent. *That's troublesome.*

"What do you know of this young lady?" the older man spat out.

"Exactly what I told you when I brought her here, sir. I witnessed her being pushed off of a wagon, and I came to her rescue."

"Look at her face," the doctor ordered.

Marshall could imagine the younger man peering at Alice.

"What about it, sir?"

"Soldier, can you tell me what color this young lady's skin is?"

"White, perhaps with a bit of tan to it?"

The doctor commanded, "Open your eyes, miss."

Silence fell for all of two seconds.

"Is she, uh, is she a Negro?" the younger man asked incredulously.

"Maybe not full-blooded, but it certainly appears that she's of African heritage. Were you aware of this?" the older man inquired accusingly.

"Sir, I swear by my mother's grave, I had no idea who or what she was."

"What of the man who you claimed pushed her from the vehicle?"

"I have no idea who he is either or where he went. I lost sight of him when I came to the girl's aid."

"What do you have to say for yourself, young lady?" the surgeon inquired.

There was no response.

"Get one of the guards," the man directed the private.

"Yes, sir."

The sound of the man scurrying out of the tent came to Marshall's ears. He had to make a quick decision. If he was going to snatch Alice from the tent, this would be the ideal time. But, even if he did manage to dislodge her from there, getting her out of the camp without being caught would prove to be nearly impossible.

As much as it irked him, he would do the prudent thing and lay low until he could find out what their plans were for her.

It took all of five minutes for Alice to be ensnared in the grasp of the guard and led to another tent, which Marshall figured was a temporary holding area for prisoners. He heard the man say that the lieutenant colonel would be calling on her at first light. The soldier shoved her inside the tent and assumed the guard position outside the door flaps.

That gave him about five hours before the commanding officer would arrive. Marshall was in a quandary. His heart wanted to concoct a plan to get Alice out of that tent and make a run for it. His head told him that by doing such a thing, he'd be setting himself up for a court-martial should they get caught. As bad as that would be for him, the situation would be grimmer for her.

There would be time enough for him to consider both options. Stealthily he made his way to the northern edge of the encampment so he could return to the Sisters of Mercy convent. On his walk there, he'd have time to weigh his options.

Arriving at the parish grounds, he wanted to check in on the children but was drawn to step into the church. The building was deserted, and the only light was from the candles flickering around the altar and the pillar offering candles set before a portrait of the Blessed Mother.

Marshall slipped into a pew, sank down to the kneeler, and made the Sign of the Cross. In his heart, he knew — regardless of the danger to himself — that he fervently desired to rescue Alice from the prison tent and escort her to safety.

That presented a moral dilemma. Would it be a sin to break his word to the Confederate Army about promising fealty to their cause? His mind wandered back to his catechism. He distinctly recalled that a mortal sin is a sin whose object is a grave matter and which is committed with full knowledge and deliberate consent. He didn't have to be a biblical scholar to know that what he planned would be done deliberately.

Might Alice's life be in jeopardy if she were sent back to Pecan Hall? He couldn't picture that situation turning out well. What if she was tortured and forced to confess where the children were? Then their lives would be at risk as well.

Does sinning to save a life justify the sin? He dropped his head into his hands. "Lord, show me the way," he intoned in a whisper.

A moment later, Marshall felt a hand on his shoulder. Startled, he glanced up and saw a priest. *Is this the answer to my prayer, Lord?*

The man nodded in greeting and then stepped into the pew and sat next to him.

"Pardon me for intruding, soldier, but I couldn't help but overhear your plea. Is there something that I can help you with?"

Marshall leaned back to the edge of the seat and regarded the man. He looked trustworthy enough, but he couldn't take any chances. He would have to hedge his bets.

"Father, would you be kind enough to hear my confession?"

"Now?"

"If you don't mind. We can even do it here if you're comfortable speaking with me face to face."

"Of course, young man." He turned to Marshall and made the Sign of the Cross over him. "*In nominee Patris, et Filii, et Spiritus Sancti. Amen.*"

"*Amen,*" echoed Marshall. Setting his jaw, he proceeded. "Bless me, Father, for I have sinned. It's been three weeks since my last confession."

From there, he prattled off the venial sins that were vexing him and then jumped headfirst into the most pressing topic. As time was of the essence, he summarized his relationship with Alice, how he'd discovered that she was of African descent and passing herself off as a Caucasian, and how she was endeavoring to save her brother and sisters when she'd been apprehended.

The priest listened intently, nodding as the story unfolded. When it came time to get to the crux of his dilemma, Marshall hesitated a moment and then let his words spill out.

"Father, I love this woman and have every intention of making her my wife when this war is resolved. We can start new lives for ourselves in Texas, where we can live independently and raise our children in freedom."

With a nod, the priest encouraged him to go on.

"As you can see, I'm wearing a Confederate uniform and have thus pledged my fealty to the Confederate Army. If I can manage to spring Alice from her entrapment, it will be considered an act of treason."

"You are right about that, son."

"Father, I feel that my duty to save Alice outweighs my loyalty to the Confederacy. Who knows, if the war continues to go as it is now, by this time next year, the Confederate union could very well be dissolved. So, my concern may be for naught."

"However, at this moment, there is still the Confederate States of America, and you are sworn to serve them," the priest reminded him.

Marshall's mouth opened, but no words came out as he struggled to control his emotions. *This isn't what I want to hear.*

"That being said," the older man added, "from my perspective, human life outweighs your allegiance to Caesar, I mean, President Jefferson Davis."

A sense of relief came to Marshall. He had to hold himself back from picking the gentleman up and giving him a bear hug.

"So, I have your blessing, sir?"

"My blessing and my prayers for your mission. There is one provision."

Marshall's heart caught in his chest. *What now?*

Chapter LI

Alice paced the interior of the square tent like a caged animal. She'd feel better if Marshall were in the vicinity, but she imagined he'd taken the children to the convent and then went back to his post.

It was up to her to concoct a believable story before the lieutenant colonel made his way there in the morning. As tired as she was, some sleep would do her good, but she had to keep her mind sharp and figure something out.

A good two hours passed, and she continued pacing, wearing out the grass beneath her feet. Pausing before the next turn around the space, a slight sound came to her ears as though someone was snapping their fingers.

Her eyes sought the source of the noise, and she nearly jumped out of her skin when she saw a hand sticking out from under the side of the tent opposite the door flaps. She stopped dead in her tracks.

Heart racing, she gave a quick prayer that it would be Marshall. The hand disappeared, and in no time flat, it was back, this time holding a velvet bag in its grasp.

Alice's knees buckled, and she fell to the ground. Crawling toward the tent wall, she reached out and grasped the hand before her. A reassuring squeeze was the response.

The bottom of the tent wall was lifted, and the hand beckoned her. Without hesitation, she fell to her stomach and inched her way hands first through the space.

Once both her arms were outside the tent, she felt them being tugged to speed the process along. Using her elbows for leverage, she squirmed the upper part of her body through the narrow opening. Marshall slid his hands under her arms and pulled her completely outside.

She wanted nothing more than to hug him for not abandoning her, but he put his fingers to his lips to silence her. Keeping low, he grabbed her hand and stealthily snaked his way through the other tents. Alice held onto him for dear life.

He must have scouted the area in advance, as they were able to steer clear of any sentries. While it took less than two minutes to vacate the encampment, it felt like an hour. Her heart was beating so loudly that she was afraid she'd awaken the sleeping soldiers as they passed by each tent.

When the camp was behind them, Marshall whispered, "Run!" And that's exactly what Alice did, sprinting as though hellhounds were nipping at her heels. Her life depended on it.

Despite the nasty stitch in her side, she kept going, not wanting to slow Marshall down. He obviously had a place in mind to take her.

A church spire came into view. It was the Sisters of Mercy parish. A sense of relief washed over her when she saw the convent. The children must be in hiding there as they'd planned.

Surprisingly though, Marshall turned off the path to the convent and kept heading toward the church. Alice hadn't enough breath to ask any questions, so she hurried alongside him and raced up the steps with him, hand in hand.

Bolting through the front door, Marshall disengaged her hand and dipped his fingers into the font to cross himself. She followed suit. That taken care of, he put his arm around her shoulder and strode to the altar, where a priest in full garb awaited them. Instinctively, they genuflected in unison.

Back on her feet, Alice's eyes opened in shock.

"Is this what I think it is?" she whispered to Marshall.

"It is if you want it to be," he replied, a sparkle in his eye.

He dropped to one knee. Alice held her hands over her face to cover her gaping mouth.

"Miss Alice," he peered at her inquiringly, "what last name do you go by anyhow?"

She glanced over at the priest. *He must think we're complete strangers*, she thought in mortification. Nonetheless, she answered. "Williams."

"Miss Alice Williams," Marshall said firmly, "will you take my hand in marriage?"

She wasn't sure if her ears were playing tricks on her, but she nodded in affirmation.

He slipped his hand into his overcoat pocket, drew out the velvet bag, emptied the contents onto his palm and then slipped the ring onto her finger.

Alice stared down at the ring in astonishment and then at the priest again.

"Now?" she squeaked out.

"It's just as good a time as any, wouldn't you say?" said Marshall with a chuckle.

"Don't we need a wit..." Before she could even get the word out, a younger priest stepped into the sanctuary, stifling a yawn with the palm of his hand.

Nodding in satisfaction, the senior priest instructed the couple to stand before him and then conducted an abbreviated wedding ceremony. As if in a dream, Alice followed along, and when it was her turn to make her vows to Marshall, she turned toward him and repeated each line after the priest.

Marshall said his vows, and the priest pronounced them husband and wife. Then her husband — as strange as that sounded — placed a sweet kiss upon her lips, sealing the promise that they'd made before God and before man.

The younger priest produced a wedding certificate, a bottle of ink and a pen, and the four of them signed on the appropriate lines to make the ceremony official. Alice read over the marriage certificate in amazement. Never in a million years would she have guessed, even a month ago, that she'd find the man of her dreams and marry him in such a short time.

Giving the priests their thanks, the two of them genuflected once again toward the altar, then Marshall grabbed her hand, and they scooted back down the aisle. On the way out of the church, they hastily dipped their fingers in the holy water and signed themselves once more.

Alice's head buzzed. She had a hundred questions for Marshall, particularly, why the rushed wedding, but that would have to wait. He grabbed her hand and sprinted toward the barn on the property, her flying a half step behind.

One question couldn't wait any longer.

"Where are we going?"

Marshall flung open the barn door, revealing Maximus, saddled and ready to go. He swung her onto the horse's back, took a seat behind her and kicked his heels into the beast's flanks to set it in motion.

"The land of opportunity," he replied loud enough to be heard over the sound of the hooves. "Texas."

Chapter LII

Not all of Marshall's spontaneous decisions in life went smoothly, but springing Alice from the camp jail, sneaking themselves into town without being detected, and getting her to marry him on the fly actually went off better than even he could have imagined.

Arms snuggled around his new wife, he set Maximus off due west in a full gallop. Speed was of the essence. He had no idea as to how long it would be before the guard realized that his prisoner had flown the coop.

It may seem impetuous to decide to settle in a territory that he'd never been to before, but all he wanted was to put Georgia — and the rest of the battleground states — behind him. Going either north or east would only put them smack dab in the center of the fighting again.

Marshall prayed that the Confederate regiment from which they were fleeing would either come to the conclusion that a young black female wasn't worth the time to pursue or would mistakenly track north.

It did worry him a bit that Cartersville could be ransacked in the soldiers' efforts to find Alice. At least her siblings were on their way to Camp Nelson. He'd made sure of that before he'd doubled back to the camp. The false bottom on the sisters' wagon would keep them concealed until they got to their destination.

The Sisters of Mercy wouldn't be giving up any secrets; he could count on that. They'd be in as much trouble as he was if they revealed that they'd been harboring fugitives. Of course, he didn't want to put them in a morally compromising position by having them lie. Hopefully, it wouldn't come to that.

With full light dawning, Marshall slowed Maximus down and maneuvered him into a batch of trees lining the side of the road. He dismounted and then helped Alice from her perch.

In their frantic rush to escape, they'd spoken hardly a word since departing the church grounds. With his wife firmly on her feet, he gathered her into his arms. She willingly fell into them, most likely as exhausted as he was.

"Did that really happen? Did we truly exchange wedding vows a few hours ago, or is this just a blissful dream?" Alice asked incredulously.

"We certainly did," he answered, looking at her tenderly. "It's a dream come true, from my perspective."

"And mine as well," she noted, sounding a bit self-conscious.

Worry came to her eyes. "Where are we to go from here, Marshall?"

"Didn't you say that Brigid knows someone who has a ranch in the eastern part of Texas? Maybe we can stay at his place for a couple of days until we get our bearings straight."

"Actually, it's that Union soldier you saw with Brigid the day that Stewart was killed. I'm not sure how he'd feel about bunking with a Confederate officer."

"Heck, once the war is done, we'll all be brothers again."

"I'm not so sure."

"Well, it doesn't hurt to extend the olive branch. What's the name of the ranch he lives on?

"Heavenly Vista. Brigid said it's located near the Red River."

"How hard could that be to find?"

"You do realize that Texas is the largest state in the Union, do you not?"

"Geography wasn't my strong suit in school, but that fact does sound familiar," said Marshall. "Even so, if God gets us that far, He certainly won't desert us there."

"True that. What about Josiah and the rest of my family? They can't stay at Camp Nelson forever. I want my son back."

"Our son," corrected Marshall with a smile.

Before he knew what hit him, Alice wrapped her arms around his waist. He returned the loving gesture. She was such a perfect fit for him. He'd be happy holding onto her forever.

Pulling back, he assured her as he gazed into her eyes. "We'll get him back, mark my words. But first, we need to put our heads together and come up with a plan for completing this leg of our journey. While it would be safer traveling at night, riding during daylight hours will be quicker."

"How many miles is it from here to the Texas border?"

"I'd say a good five hundred."

"And how many miles can a horse with two riders cover in a day?"

"Somewhere between twenty-five and thirty-five."

"The median number is thirty miles a day. So, we're

talking a little more than two weeks of travel. Seventeen days to be more precise, assuming that the horse stays in stable health."

Hearing her calculating figures in her head, Marshall's eyebrows shot up admiringly.

"We've twice as much daylight as we do night cover, so it only makes sense to travel during the day. If we act above suspicion, would anyone question us?"

"Your guess is as good as mine, little lady."

He considered her proposal. It seemed sound. Now they just needed to have a story to explain why a confederate soldier was traveling on horseback with a young lady. *Out for a joyride probably won't fly.*

"You're good at subterfuge, Alice. How shall we present ourselves if anyone accosts us?"

"That's something that will take more consideration. If I wear my widow clothing, will it cause raised eyebrows if I'm sharing a saddle with you?

"I'm afraid it might," he responded. "We need to determine which garb will be the least conspicuous. Besides the black dress and veil, you have a day dress, correct? I've got my uniform, but I can pack the jacket and slouch hat away to blend in more readily."

Alice's eyes shifted upwards as she considered the options. Finally, she gave her assessment. "I believe we'd have less cause to be stopped if you stayed in your uniform. As for myself, I'll switch out of the black and into the other dress. It doesn't stand out as much."

"How will we explain our relationship?"

"We'll say we're brother and sister. The family home was destroyed in the crossfire of a battle on our property. You've been granted leave to take me to our relative's home somewhere. We'll make up a town if we need to."

She looked up into his eyes. "Does that sound like a reasonable plan to you?"

"Reasonable, yes. Playing the part of your brother may be an arduous endeavor seeing that I can't take my eyes off of you."

The blush that came to Alice's face caused Marshall to break out in laughter.

"What am I going to do with you?" she asked, starting to laugh herself.

"We'll see soon enough," he replied, his eyes crinkling with merriment.

Chapter LIII

They'd only traveled a couple hours, but Alice's derriere was already feeling the effects of the horseback ride. Even though she'd grown up on a plantation and had been around horses her whole life, she'd never actually ridden one until today.

All in all, the trip was a pleasant one. She and Marshall chatted comfortably as they went along. She loved hearing stories of his formative years. He'd certainly given his mother a run for her money.

It sounded as though he was always the life of the party. The jokes that he relayed had her in stitches as the horse kept at its steady pace. Between anecdotes and stories, he was wont to burst into song. *Be still my beating heart!* She was mesmerized by his singing.

The sweet thing about Marshall was that as much as he enjoyed speaking of his escapades, he seemed generally interested in her life as well. After some prodding, she relayed to him the story of her royal heritage.

He absorbed her tale thoughtfully.

"Princess," he finally said, "would you mind indulging me and answering more questions about your life?"

She wrinkled her nose at him, eyes twinkling. "Seeing that you're my knight in shining armor and you've saved the day, be my guest," she replied haughtily.

He went on to grill her on the countless topics of

study that she'd undertaken in her years of schooling.

"Marshall, I'm more than happy to oblige you and answer your questions," she stated, "but surely you must have studied all those things yourself in school."

"I would imagine I did, but the rambling from those stodgy old teachers went in one ear and out the other," he admitted. "For some reason, hearing these same facts from your lips is much more intriguing."

Her cheeks grew flushed. "As clever as you are, I can't imagine that you were a poor student."

"You know those fellows who were at the top of their class?"

She nodded expectantly.

"I was in the group that helped place them there."

Alice rolled her eyes. *The things this man says. I'll be forever on my toes.*

Marshall continued, "My father told me on more than one occasion, 'Son, you have the ability to do anything you put your mind to.' But only a few topics actually caught my interest enough to keep me engaged."

"Such as..." she encouraged.

"War, political science, music."

That explained his singing skills.

"Still, you must have gotten acceptable grades."

"Acceptable to me? Yes. To my father? No. That was until I decided to apply to The Citadel. Then I finally put my nose to the grindstone."

"Timing is everything, as they say. See how well that turned out?"

He gave no reply, which caused Alice to glance behind her to see what was the matter.

Marshall sat straight up in the saddle, looking as

though he were straining to hear something. She leaned her head to see past him and saw two Confederate soldiers on horseback coming up on them from behind.

At the speed the men were traveling, she couldn't determine if they meant to pass them or stop them. It took less than a minute to find out. Sensing their horses pulling up alongside Maximus, instinctively, she pulled her rosary beads from the pocket of her dress. She had her share of talents, but lying wasn't one of them. She'd let Marshall do the talking.

"Excuse us, solider," said one of the men. "Would you mind stopping for a moment?"

Immediately Marshall pulled on the reins to bring the animal to a halt. He turned and saluted the superior officer.

"May I help you?" he addressed the men solicitously.

"My partner and I are patrolling these roads. It's unusual to run across a soldier in this neck of the woods that we don't recognize. Can you tell us what business you're about?"

"Of course, Captain. I've been granted leave to bring my sister to our kin in Western Arkansas. She's a bit traumatized. Unfortunately, our home was caught in a crossfire during a skirmish in northern Georgia. Yanks burned it to the ground."

"Sorry to hear that, soldier. Would you mind showing us your papers with said orders?"

"Certainly."

Alice kept her head down, seemingly concentrating on her rosary beads, so the two men wouldn't get a clear view of her face. Marshall made a show of digging through his overcoat pockets.

"Well, I'll be darned. I swore I put those papers here."

"Perhaps they're in the saddlebags?" the officer suggested.

"Could be." Marshall swung his leg off the horse and opened each saddlebag and dug through the contents. "Wonder if I misplaced them at our last stop."

The horses seemed to be getting impatient, their riders no doubt as well.

"What's your name?" the soldier in charge inquired.

"First Lieutenant Marshall Kent. Sir, my aunt's waiting for my sister to be delivered to her doorstep. We're not more than a day's ride out. The minute she's delivered, I'm heading back to my post."

"Well, First Lieutenant Kent, as much as I can sympathize with your situation, I can't allow you to continue with no papers. If you've lost them, they need to be reissued. We can take care of that back at our headquarters in Brownsville."

"That's most kind. But, how about we do this? We're not too far from Little Rock. I can drop Alais off at the Catholic church there. I would imagine the sisters in the convent would be generous enough to put her up for a bit until I get this paperwork squared away."

"Sounds reasonable enough," the officer replied. "Just to be on the safe side, we'll accompany you there and then back to our headquarters."

Alice felt Marshall tense up. Obviously, that wasn't the solution that he'd hoped for. Regardless, he answered back in the affirmative. "That's very accommodating of you, sir."

The trio of horses continued westward. With Maximus a few paces ahead of the other two mounts,

Marshall whispered into Alice's ear.

"I'll get you situated at the convent. Maybe you can offer to teach at the parish school in exchange for room and board until I get back."

"How long will that be?"

"Best-case scenario, a couple days. Worst-case, it could be a couple of months until I worm my way out of the grasp of the Confederate Army."

That answer didn't sit well with her.

"Who knows," he added reassuringly, "perhaps the rumors are true, and Jefferson Davis is looking for terms of surrender. If that's the case, before we know it, the war will be over and, with that, my commitment to serve in the Confederate Army will be fulfilled."

Even a couple of days apart seemed too long to Alice, but the situation was out of her hands. Her heart sank lower as they approached the church grounds.

"Promise me something," directed Marshall.

"Anything," she said in a choked voice.

"Wait for me until I get back."

Tears spilling down her cheeks, Alice nodded in agreement.

Chapter LIV

It took every bit of Marshall's persuasion techniques to convince the commanding officer at the headquarters in Brownsville that he hadn't been attempting to desert the Confederate Army. He managed to avoid getting thrown into the brig but still wasn't off the hook.

Marshall detailed his role in the army, training fresh recruits, but they were disinterested, to put it mildly. From their perspective, the Reb army needed more men on the battlefield and less commanding from the rear. Thus, he was assigned to their regiment and by the next day was traipsing toward Memphis with his fellow soldiers.

Their goal was to meet up with Lieutenant General William J. Hardee's Department of South Carolina, Georgia and Florida. Hood had taken the bulk of forces in Georgia on his campaign to Tennessee with the hope that Sherman would divert from his March to the Sea and pursue them.

Marshall wasn't sure how he felt about being the carrot dangled in front of Sherman's nose, but it was all for naught anyhow. Hood's tactical maneuver turned out to be a bust. With Atlanta under control of Union forces, Sherman and his men started their march south to the Gulf of Mexico on the fifteenth of November.

As soon as Hood got word of that, he set his troops after the major general. This consisted of thirteen-thousand men who'd been holed up at Lovejoy's Station, south of Atlanta, a couple thousand of Major General Gustavus W. Smith's Georgia militia soldiers — if you could call boys and old men such a thing — and the Calvary Corp of Major General Joseph Wheeler, reinforced by a brigade under Brigadier General William H. Jackson, a total of ten-thousand.

With forces a third the size of Sherman's, the Confederates didn't have enough strength to overpower the Union Army but did have enough troops to nip at their heels as they made their way south.

The term "total war" had meant nothing to Marshall until he witnessed the devastation that Sherman left in his wake. Following a "scorched earth" policy, his forces destroyed military targets as well as infrastructure, industry and civilian property — disrupting the Southern economy and transportation networks.

Loyalty to the Confederate cause grew thin on Marshall's behalf as time wore on. The longer they trailed after the Union troops, the more pointless the whole exercise seemed. He guessed that some of the other fellows around him were of a like mindset but, like him, dared not speak out and be branded a traitor.

Hardly a moment went by that Alice wasn't in his thoughts. They'd been married all of ten hours before they were torn apart again. Thankfully, she was safe and sound at the Sisters of Mercy Convent in Little Rock. He knew she'd be able to fend for herself until he returned to her.

Sherman captured the port of Savannah, Georgia, on the twenty-first of December. The end of the war seemed to be in sight.

From a military standpoint, 1864 had certainly proven to be a memorable one for Marshall. He'd started out in a relatively safe post, but as the year marched on, he was in the line of fire on nearly a daily basis.

It hadn't taken him more than a day in the field to realize that drilling men to fight was a whole lot different than being in the thick of the battle himself. He thought back to all the soldiers that he'd trained through the years. What fate had befallen them?

Until he got to heaven, he'd never know. Not that he was in any hurry to get there though. His number one priority was to stay alive and reunite with Alice. And he used every trick in the book to do so.

Chapter LV

As much as Alice's heart ached for Marshall, she felt secure residing with the Sisters of Mercy. Through the strangest set of circumstances, Miss Brigid McGinnis was there as well. After what she'd witnessed between that young lady and the Union soldier back in Cartersville, it was a surprise seeing her dressed as a postulant. But, not wanting to pry into her private matters, she kept her thoughts and questions to herself.

Alice had a renewed sense of purpose in living amongst the sisters. They were more than happy to have another teacher at the school that they ran for the local orphans.

Surprisingly, her heritage seemed to be of little interest to the good women. Or the students, for that matter. The little faces that greeted her each morning were a rainbow of colors. Her classroom consisted of Caucasian, Negro and Indian children from the orphanage.

One little boy particularly tugged at her heartstrings. Silas had been abandoned as a newborn. He seemed to be quite bright. At only four years old, he was already beginning to read.

Maybe it was because he reminded her of herself at that age, or because he was a mulatto with her same skin coloring, but over the months, he'd come to feel like a son to her. It helped soothe her sorrow over missing Josiah.

When Alice wasn't teaching, she was in church

praying for Marshall. She refused to leave the safety of the parish grounds. There was no use tempting fate.

After the first week had passed with no word from him, she knew that she was in it for the long haul. If he had been reassigned, he would be with his unit until the hostilities came to an end.

Alice absorbed every bit of war news that she could get her hands on. Most came from listening to the prayer intentions that Father offered at Mass each morning. People prayed for their sons, their brothers, or their husbands, who were serving with various units throughout the South.

Initially, the prayers centered on the Confederate Army winning the war, but in time, they shifted to pleading that the war would cease and that all the men would be able to come home to their loved ones. She never voiced her intentions out loud, but the latter was precisely what Alice prayed for.

Days turned into weeks and weeks into months with no word from Marshall. Alice threw herself into the task of educating the children in her charge. As much as she loved working with the students in the lower grades, when it was discovered that she had a broad education in advanced subjects, she was transferred to a classroom with upper-level pupils.

Enlightening children's minds and introducing them to worlds of which they hadn't been aware was gratifying work. By osmosis, her passion for learning was absorbed by the children. As she had no idea how long she'd be teaching there, she wanted to pass along every bit of knowledge to them that she could before she moved on.

On April 9, 1865, seven months after she'd arrived in

Little Rock, the Battle of Appomattox Court House in Virginia, which lasted only a few hours, was the death knell to the Confederate States. It led to General Robert E. Lee's surrender of his Army of Northern Virginia to Union General Ulysses S. Grant.

It had taken several days for the news to reach them in Arkansas, but when Father made the announcement before Mass that Sunday morning, the entire church broke out into raucous cheering with the sound of weeping interspersed between the clapping, whistling and shouting.

Alice could have wept for joy herself.

Now, it was just a matter of waiting for Marshall to return. She had no idea how the logistics of dismantling an army went, so she put every ounce of energy she possessed into her students, sweeping them along in a tidal wave of knowledge.

One afternoon in early May, she had her back to the class as she tapped the African continent on a world map, with the children saying the name of each country from north to south. Just as she got to the southernmost country, the room went silent.

A voice came from the back. "South Africa."

The pointer slipped from Alice's fingers and noisily bounced off the floor. She whirled around. Every eye in the room was on the soldier standing in the doorway. Without thinking, she picked up her skirts and raced to the man.

She threw her arms around his neck. "Marshall! Is it really you?"

"In the flesh," he replied jauntily.

He swept his hat off his head and placed a kiss soundly on Alice's lips.

"Oooohhh," said a sea of voices in unison.

Feeling a bit foolish, Alice swung around to face her students.

"May I introduce my husband, First Lieutenant Marshall Kent."

"Make that, Captain Marshall Kent."

The students politely stood up and welcomed him. Alice dismissed class early. As the overjoyed students bounded out the door, she looked at Marshall, her eyes sparkling in delight.

"You're my star student today."

"By chance, I happened to walk in just as you were pointing to the only country in Africa that I could identify," he said with a laugh.

"Guess I have my work cut out for me catching you up," Alice retorted.

"Good thing we have a lifetime ahead of us to do so, my love."

Epilogue

Marshall and Alice took their time getting to Texas. They were enjoying life as newlyweds, even though, in reality, they'd been married close to a year.

Their destination was Heavenly Vista Ranch. Alice had written to Brigid and was assured by both her and her husband Dominic that they would be welcome to stay on the property until they decided where they wanted to settle.

Thankfully, they'd been able to secure a wagon for the trip. Alice didn't know if she could have taken that much time on the back of a horse.

Cresting the hill on the edge of the Heavenly Vista property, Alice had been overwhelmed by the view before them. A good-sized house, a barn, stables, a herd of cattle grazing. It was idyllic, something she'd only seen in picture books before.

Beyond that, a town was forming on the horizon. A church with a tall steeple was nearly complete, another building was under construction and beyond that, several houses dotted the landscape.

A crowd of people had gathered at the main house to welcome them. To Alice's delight and utter amazement, Brigid was there, no longer a postulant but the wife of Sergeant Dominic Warner.

Then there was Dominic's business partner Nathan and his wife Amara, Amara's brother Michael and his spouse Josephine, Josephine's brother Hubert, his bride Bernadette, an older Hispanic couple, Eduardo and Maria, a Cherokee Indiana named Saligugi, who went by his English moniker, Snapping Turtle, and Ol' Joe, a free black.

Soon enough, their numbers would be increasing, she discerned from glancing at the silhouettes of Amara, Brigid and Josephine, who were in various stages of pregnancy. She smiled, thinking of her own family, who would soon be arriving from Camp Nelson.

Alice and Marshall had been assured from the moment they arrived that they were welcome to stay at the ranch as long as they'd like or join their growing community if they were of a mind to.

Planting their roots in this peaceful valley sounded ideal to both her and Marshall.

Thankfully, Marcus had made it through the war unharmed, and he could transport the rest of Alice's family to Texas as well. Abraham and Josiah would have a whole set of friends close to their age when they arrived. Her heart felt close to bursting as she thought of holding her little boy in her arms again.

It would take a while to get everyone's names straight, but they all lived in close proximity to Nathan and Amara, so she and Marshall would see everyone enough to get to know them personally.

Nathan and Dominic were in the process of incorporating their community. The night they'd first arrived, the adults sat down for a late supper and discussed the plans that the men had sketched out.

Alice could hardly believe her ears. The group talked of a town where people of all races would live together in harmony. With an abundance of natural resources close at hand, they could start a lumber business and a mill. Industry and faith would be the lifeblood of their community.

Each person had their strengths and talents and was willing to work to create this municipality. For once in her life, Alice felt completely at home. Marshall could put his law degree to good use here. With her extensive education, she would contribute in whatever way she saw fit, whether it was teaching or helping her husband with his practice.

Energy flowed through the room as ideas were deliberated and debated. At the end of the night, the discussion wound down, leaving just one topic left to cover. If they were going to incorporate their community in the state of Texas, they'd have to have a name for it.

Seeing that Nathan and Dominic had first claimed this stake, it could be named after one or the other of them, something along the line of Simmons or Warner, or a derivative of that. Neither man felt comfortable with that kind of recognition, though.

Despite the fact that she barely knew the people surrounding her, Alice was inspired to speak out.

"May I offer a suggestion?"

"Of course," said Nathan.

"I've heard of communities started by freed slaves, particularly in Texas, called freedmen towns. As our municipality will be comprised of people of a variety of races, how would you feel about calling it Freedom?"

The men and women sitting on the benches lining the dining room table looked from one person to another. Chattering picked up as the name was discussed.

"All in favor?" noted Dominic.

Every hand raised in approval.

"Freedom it is," shouted Michael over the din.

Marshall stood up, gathered Alice into his arms, and swung her around in a circle, joy evident on both their faces. "Freedom. A freedom such as heaven intended. Sounds perfect to me." He bestowed a kiss on her lips.

"Awww..." said the other young ladies in one voice.

For once, Alice didn't care what other people thought. She wrapped her arms around Marshall's neck and kissed him back just as soundly.

It really was perfect. As was her life, thanks to God and his heavenly hosts for their intercession on her behalf. The dimples in Alice's cheeks deepened as she smiled brightly at her husband, the man with whom she'd vowed to have and to hold until death doth they part. And beyond that. For eternity.

Acknowledgments

For my husband of 40 years, John Lauer, our children Stephanie, Nicholas, Samantha and Elizabeth, their families, and our entire extended family for their continual love and support;

For Cinnamin Drexel, who is not only our beautiful cover model but also the inspiration for our female protagonist Alice;

For The Citadel graduate Gerald Toney whose insight into life at The Citadel was invaluable in creating the back story for our male protagonist Marshall;

For The Most Reverend Donald Zuleger, who claims that I'm his favorite Catholic author, for help with theological questions that arose during the writing of this book;

For Fr. Edward Looney, who was able to clarify moral questions concerning Confession;

For Egide Nimubona, for clarifying to me the history of his home country Burundi and the continent of Africa;

For Betsy Ross, who shared her knowledge of horse terminology with me;

For photographer Brad Birkholz, who shot the photo of our cover model and the barns on both the front and back covers;

For Sue Kiesau who provided the Civil War-era gown for our cover model;

For James Hrkach, who created an entrancing book cover that immediately draws readers into this Civil War romance;

For my publisher Ellen Gable Hrkach whose continued faith and confidence in me and my work inspires me to keep writing;

For my publisher, Full Quiver Publishing, which is dedicated to publishing novels that will entertain, enlighten and bring readers closer to Christ;

To all the soldiers who fought in the Civil War — all gave some; some gave all.

About the Author

Amanda Lauer is the author of the best-selling *Heaven Intended* Civil War series. *A World Such as Heaven Intended* won the 2016 YA CALA award. Lauer won Best Writer 2020 (Red Letter Awards) for her work on the movie *The Islands*. She collaborated on the recently released children's book *Dubbie: The Double-Headed Eagle.* Her time-travel novel, *Anything But Groovy*, was published in February 2021. Her story *Lucky and Blessed*, part of the anthology *Treasures: Visible & Invisible*, was released on March 1, 2021. Over the last twenty years, Lauer has had nearly 1,600 articles published in newspapers and magazines throughout the United States. She and her husband John have been married forty years and have four grown children, two sons-in-law, a daughter-in-law, and seven remarkable grandchildren.

Published by
Full Quiver Publishing
PO Box 244
Pakenham ON K0A2X0
Canada
www.fullquiverpublishing.com

Made in USA - Kendallville, IN
72125_9781987970319
11.04.2021 1251